The
Battle

Charlotte Maria Tucker

Eirenikos Press

ISBN: 9781520714288

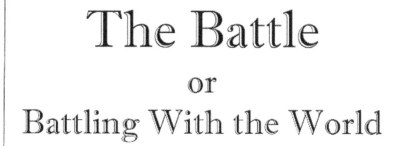

The Battle

or
Battling With the World

by Charlotte Maria Tucker

Illustrator Unknown

Preface

I have ventured to hope that the young readers of "The Giant-killer" might be disposed to welcome a little volume which should tell them of the further fortunes of dome of the friends with whom they made acquaintance in that work. Fides himself is absent from my picture; I have dropped the veil of allegory altogether, and present my readers with a simple sketch of such quiet home-trials and home-sorrows as some of them may already have experienced. The champion himself appears no more, but he has left behind him his wondrous sword, which I would fain, though conscious of feebleness in the attempt, teach some of his young followers to wield. I hope that the poetry which I have introduced more freely into this than into any other of tales may not render it less acceptable to the young. The headings to the chapters have almost entirely been taken from a small volume of my poems; entitled "Glimpses of the Unseen;" the hymns have not before appeared in print.

CONTENTS

The Roby Family Series

The Giant Killer

The Battle

Other Books by Charlotte Maria Tucker

The Robbers Cave

The Young Pilgrim

Hebrew Heroes

The Crown of Success

The Mine or Darkness and Light

1. Selfishness and Self-Denial

No weapon we own,
But the sword of the Spirit;
And Mercy alone,
Shall the kingdom Inherit!

Now, Con, I should just like to know what you are thinking about?"
cried Adolphus, Probyn, as he dropped one lump of sugar after another
into his cup of warm chocolate, and skimmed off the mantling surface with
the air of an epicure. "I should like to know what you are thinking about.
You look as grave and as solemn as a judge!"

"I was, very naturally, thinking of the poor Robys," replied his brother.

"Ah!" exclaimed Adolphus, "how little we know what will happen! How
little we thought, when we drove from the green gate at Dove's Nest, and
left so many happy, smiling faces behind us, and expected to see them again
in a month, that, long before that month should be over, one of the party
would be dead, and the others so miserable and wretched."

"Mr. Roby certainly looked ill," observed Constantine; "but I never
dreamed, when he addressed as that last morning after prayers, that I
should never hear his voice again. It seems as though his death had stamped
ail those last words more deeply upon my mind!" The boy's tone faltered a
little as he spoke.

"Yes; I remember very well about the foes in our hearts (the giants Mrs.
Roby would have called them), against whom we were all to do battle."

"And our swords — our Bibles," rejoined Constantine. "Don't you
recollect, Adolphus that our occupation on our last Sunday at Dove's Nest

was making a list of the sins that beset us, and finding out a verse to use against each?"

"Well, somehow or other," said Adolphus, "they managed to make Sunday pass pleasantly enough there. We seemed getting into the quiet ways of the good folks; and I'm really sorry that Mr. Roby is dead, for I'm afraid that we'll now be sent to school."

Constantine gave a look more expressive than polite, on hearing the selfish nature of his brother's regrets; but, without taking further notice of it said, "Have you kept the paper which you wrote on that last Sunday?"

"Oh, not I! What between the corrections and the blottings, it was not worth the keeping. I don't pretend to write as cleverly as Aleck."

"I have kept mine," said his brother, gravely, "and marked all the verses in my Bible besides They will always remind me of the Robys and Dove's Nest."

"What a happy party they used to be there!" cried Adolphus,

"I am afraid that we did not add much to their happiness. I, at least, was a terrible plague to poor Bertha. I believe that she would, at one time, have done anything to have got rid of my company. Poor little thing! She has worse trials now."

"They'll all have to leave Dove's Nest," observed Adolphus.

"Really!" said Constantine, looking earnestly at his brother. "Are they, then, so very poor?"

"Oh! Dreadfully poor," was the reply.

"How do you know that?" inquired Con.

"Was I not with Aunt Lawrence yesterday evening, and did I not hear all about it? Did she not give me the black-edged letter from poor Mrs., Roby to read?"

"Oh, I wish that I had seen it! What did she write?" exclaimed Constantine, edging his chair nearer to his brother's.

"She wrote thanking my aunt for kindness and sympathy. The paper looked blotted and blistered. I think that she had been crying over it; but the words were very submissive: there was not a syllable of complaint."

"What she must have suffered! — Such a devoted wife as she was! And her loss so terribly sudden!"

"Then she went on to ask if my aunt could assist her in procuring some situation as governess." "As governess!" exclaimed Constantine; "then she must be poor indeed! To think of her ever coming to that!"

"She wrote, 'I have three dear children depending on my exertions. I must now live and work to support them.' "

"Poor Mrs. Roby!" cried Constantine, with feeling; "it is enough quite to break her heart! She has been placed in the furnace indeed, and heavy, crushing blows have fallen upon her. How could she bear to leave her children? They are all that are left to her now."

"Better leave them and work, than stay with them and starve."

"Aleck is more than thirteen, and might do some thing," exclaimed Constantine. "If I had a mother and such a mother as he has, I'd rather work my arms from their sockets than let her go out among strangers!"

"Working his arms from their sockets is quite out of the way of such a clever young gentleman as Aleck!" The heart of Adolphus smote him at his own words, though he had not taken enough of trouble in self-examination to know what petty envy and malice had prompted them.

"I should like to know," said Constantine, after a pause, "what my aunt replied to Mrs. Roby."

"I told you that I knew all about it. Aunt Lawrence told her of a situation."

"Where? — Where?" interrupted his brother.

"At Lady Bunnington's, in Grosvenor Place: she has just parted with her governess."

"What sort of a woman is Lady Bunnington, I wonder?"

"I fancy, from what Aunt Lawrence said, a gay, dashing sort of person.

3

There are a whole set of little Buns, I believe." Adolphus leaned back and laughed at his own wit, but Con was too much interested to be merry."

"After the quiet, happy, useful life of a clergy man's wife in the country," he said, "to come as a stranger, a dependant, into a bustling, crowded city, when her grief is so recent, too, and so great! And will she leave all her children behind her?"

"There was something more in my aunt's letter," said Adolphus, with the air of one who is a party to a secret.

"Money?" suggested Constantine. "I don't know about that. I should rather think, from Mrs. Roby's grateful expressions, that Aunt Lawrence had not waited till now to send that,"

"She's a good creature, after all, our Aunt Lawrence!" cried Constantine; "and yet we used to dislike her, and think her so horridly particular."

"Well, I shouldn't like to live with her now," said Adolphus; "but it's different with one of the Robys."

"One of the Robys! What do you mean?" "Why, Aunt Lawrence has offered, in her letter, to take charge of one of the little girls."

"You don't say so!" cried Constantine with animation,

"I do say so; she told me so herself I've no doubt that Mrs., Roby will be only too glad to accept the offer. I only hope that she'll send little Laura, she's such a pretty, merry, jolly little puss!"

"Well, I don't know; I feel more for poor Bertha, she is so very, very fond of her mother. I think that the parting would be worse for her; and, of courier, if Mrs. Roby is governess in Grosvenor Place, she will have many opportunities of going to Aunt Lawrence's and seeing her daughter there. I say, 'Dolphus," said Constantine, leaning forward, as if a sudden thought had struck him, "I wonder if we could do anything for the family of our poor tutor. We owe much more to him and to them than Aunt Lawrence does, or ever did."

"Oh, they were paid for it all!" said Adolphus.

"Paid for our board, lodging, and teaching — yes," replied Constantine; "but there are some things which could never be paid for, — all the pains which they took with our characters; their anxiety to lead us in the road to heaven, so gently, so patiently, so wisely. They first taught us to think, to feel, to know our own faults, and the way to straggle against them; and I am sure," he added, more earnestly, laying his clenched hand on the table, "that if we ever turn out anything better than the selfish, self-willed idlers that we were, we owe it to the two years that we have passed in the quiet home of the Robys."

"We do them mighty credit, no doubt!" cried Adolphus, laughing.

"Gratitude!" continued Constantine, without noticing the interruption — "I once should have been ashamed to have owned that I felt it; I never thought of a kindness when it was past; but I have learned that it is selfish pride not to be sensible of an obligation, and petty meanness not to acknowledge it."

"Spoken like a book!" cried Adolphus. "I think that you must have got up that sentence for the occasion. Well, we may be grateful, and I am grateful for kindness. I'm not too proud to say so; and there's an end of the matter."

"But how can we prove our gratitude?" asked his brother.

"We've both written to Dove's Nest already."

"But we have sent nothing."

"What have we to send? Shall I buy a box of sugar-plums for Laura?"

"I wish you had some sense in you!" cried Constantine impatiently.

"I wish you had some manners in you!" retorted his brother.

Constantine had risen from his seat, and sauntered to the fireplace, not for the sake of warmth, for the month was July, and gold shavings instead of hot coals glittered in the grate; but he leaned his hand against the marble mantelpiece, and appeared buried in thought. Adolphus, having finished his breakfast, amused himself with spinning a shilling on the table. Constantine was the first to break the silence.

"Pro," said he, for he often addressed his brother by the familiar name which the young Robys had given him — "Pro, I'm thinking that next Tuesday is our birthday."

5

"Well, that's odd! My thoughts were running on just the same thing at that moment. I was considering that we ought to have roly-poly for dinner."

Constantine's smile was a little contemptuous. "Or rather, as there are two of us, two roly-poly," said pro — "one of plum-jam, the other of pineapple!"

"Do you remember what papa promised to give as on our birthday?"

"Don't I! Why, we're each to have a gold watch! A famous thing for us it will be!"

"Now, Pro," said Constantine, resuming his seat by his brother, "those watches will cost a great deal of money."

"Lots!" cried Adolphus, tossing up his shilling.

"Suppose," continued Constantine, softening his tone — "suppose that we were to ask papa to send that money to Mrs. Roby instead."

"Suppose that we do no such thing," replied Pro; slipping his shilling into his waistcoat pocket.

"Would you not like to help our friends in their distress?"

"Very much indeed," said the boy, "if I could do so without trouble or loss to myself. But we must always consider Number One, and I've no notion of giving up my watch."

"Adolphus, you're in the pit of selfishness, and you'll stay there all your life," cried his brother with scowl.

"I'll make myself comfortable in it, at least; I was never meant for a hero," said Adolphus, as he strolled carelessly out of the room, and Constantine heard him the next minute whistling on the stairs.

There is much in the force of example; and Constantine, though for the first moment he felt indignant at the selfishness of his brother, began before long to view matters in a different light.

"Well, after all, I don't see that we are called upon to make so great a sacrifice for the Robys. I have been looking forward for the last year to having a watch of my own. I never wished so much for anything before. How I shall like to wear it, to listen to its ticking, to wind it, to examine its works! A watch looks so gentlemanly, too. I hope that papa intends to add a gold chain."

Constantine stuck his thumb into his waistcoat pocket, and raised his head with a boorish air, fancying the ornament already gracing his neck. "I'm certainly very sorry for the Robys, but they never expect money from me. I'll write another note to Bertha, and say all that I can think of to comfort her. I am sure that she will consider that very kind." He unlocked his rosewood desk, opened it, and proceeded to look for materials for writing.

The first paper on which Constantine laid his hand was that which he had written on his last Sunday at Dove's Nest. Pride, sloth, untruth, hate, fee, appeared down the page, and opposite to each some verse from Scripture chosen by himself as his weapon against them. He had unintentionally unsheathed "the sword of the Spirit," and a bright ray of truth flashed from it upon his soul. Beside the name of selfishness were written the words, Inasmuch as ye did it unto the least of these, my brethren, ye did it unto me. Constantine sat down, and leaned his head thoughtfully upon his hand.

"How strange that I should light upon that paper!" thought he. "The sight of it has brought so vividly to my mind the whole scene of the Sunday reading at Dove's Nest — the party assembled in that dear little parlor, the great picture Bible open on the table, the red light of the setting sun streaming in through the narrow latticed windows upon that face which I shall behold no more!

He looked so holy, and yet so bright, I might have guessed that he was very near heaven. When he had read out that verse he laid the paper down, and said, in his deep earnest tone "(Constantine could not recall the exact words, but their sense had left a deep impression behind), " ' My children, let us dwell on that sentence. When, by whom, and to whom will it be spoken? It will be uttered when heaven and earth pass away, when the myriads of the dead shall arise from their graves, when before the white throne of the eternal Judge countless multitudes shall stand. It shall be uttered by that Judge himself, arrayed in his awful glory, upon whose smile or frown our endless bliss or misery shall hang! And to whom will that sentence be uttered, that gracious remembrance of the smallest act of kindness rendered to the feeblest of his children? '

Mr. Roby clasped his hands, looked silently on those round him, and then added, rather as if praying than as addressing them, ' God grant that it may be uttered to each one of us! "It seemed to me then," mused Constantine, "as if the joy of hearing these words from the lips of my. Judge, ' Come, ye blessed of my Father,' would be worth the sacrifice of everything on earth!" Softened feeling moistened the eye of the boy: like flowers that shed perfume over the grave, the remembrance of his departed friend was sweet, and left the fragrance of holiness behind.

"I wonder if I could recollect the verses of the others," mused Constantine. "No; I can only remember one, and that was Laura's, written in a very large round hand, Lay up for yourselves treasures in heaven. She was sitting next her father, I know, and he laid his hand fondly on her curly head; I think that I can see them now. 'It is not,' he said, ' that we can earn merit for anything that we do; we are unprofitable servants, poor pardoned sinners, owing all that we have to mercy; yet the Lord deigns, for his only Son's sake, to accept our poor attempts to serve him; not one kind deed, not one kind word, is lost or forgotten by him, and even a little child like my Laura may begin to lay up treasure in heaven.'

Ah, kind, generous Mr. Roby, what treasures he had laid up for himself, and now he has gone to enjoy them! How he denied himself for others — how he spared neither labor nor time — how he fed the hungry, and visited the sick, and was loaded with the blessings of the poor! While I — what have I ever done, what have I ever attempted to do, to please God or to serve a fellow- creature? I grudge giving up a single indulgence for those who were so kind and good to me — for those who are in such deep sorrow — for the family of one of God's holiest servants! What if, when the Lord comes in his glory, he should say to me, Inasmuch as ye did it not unto them, ye did it not unto me?" As the thought glanced through the mind of Constantine, he hastily quitted the apartment

The Battle (Illustrated)

2. Rebellion and Submission

Affliction to a pious mind
Is like the rough, tempestuous wind
Which sweeps the Eolian harp, and there
Wakes but the melody of prayer!

We will now change the scene to Dove's Nest. How different a place from what it was when the Probyns first visited that peaceful home! True, the scent of the sweet-brier is fragrant as ever; the songs of the birds, the tinkle of the sheep- bell, the hum of the bees, is still heard; and the clustering roses peep in at the lattice, looking as bright and as fresh as in happier days. But within the cottage all is altered. There is scarcely a voice or a footfall heard; the clock in the stillness seems to tick too loud; there are numbers on the old familiar articles of furniture which mark them out as things to be sold; the framed drawings, the worked screen, nay, even that venerated chair which always now stands empty in its place — all — all are to be parted with to strangers! The poor orphans wander from room to room, speaking, when tears will let them speak, of the past, now never to be recalled, and the unknown dreaded future before them.

It is now the hour of breakfast. The family, dressed in deep mourning, are assembled in the parlor to partake of a very frugal meal. None appear to have appetite for it but poor little Laura, who is almost ashamed of feeling so hungry. Mrs. Roby occupies her usual seat. All the color is fled from her cheek, all the sparkle gone from her eye; her thin hand trembles as she prepares the meal, but she is too unselfish in her sorrow to give free course to her grief She is still thinking of every one, caring for every one, fearful of casting any added gloom on the young hearts of her father less children. Her own is very, very heavy; but still she never murmurs, and seldom weeps, except when alone with her God.

Breakfast proceeds for some time in silence, except for a remark from the mother that the post is unusually late. There is evidently some letter expected with anxiety, perhaps with fear. Mrs. Roby almost dreads the success of her own efforts to procure a situation as governess, and her children regard with unmixed distress the idea of being separated from her. Oh, how many whispered consultations have Aleck and Bertha held in private together! How the poor boy has wished and longed to be older, to be able to do something for himself, and help his widowed mother, instead of being, as now, a burden upon her! How many schemes he has thought over, and talked over with Bertha, for gaining money, by teaching, copying out, writing books, as he has read of others doing before him! But no path seems open to Aleck, for his extreme youth is a barrier before all: he cannot teach without pupils; no one whom he knows requires to have manuscripts copied; and as for authorship — poor boy! Though his writings may serve to amuse his sisters on a winter's evening, even vanity cannot blind his eyes to the fact that no one would give a farthing for them all.

Bertha's schemes are of a humbler description; she thinks not of what she might earn, but of how little she could live on; — how her clothes by constant mending should last her for ever; how she never would cost her poor mother one shilling which, by the strictest self-denial, could be saved. But her plans seem as fruitless as her brother's. She cannot avoid being an expense to one who will have to depend on her own efforts for bread. Food must be purchased, decent mourning bought, some shelter provided for the helpless children so soon to be driven from their once happy home.

Laura is the only one of the party too young to be oppressed by care, though she laments, like a child, all the treasured things she will now be obliged to part with.

"Bertie," she whispered softly to her sister at breakfast, "must all these pretty cups and saucers be sold too?"

Bertha raised her finger to her lips, and gave a glance towards her mother to silence the little questioner.

"What will we drink our tea out of then?" again whispered Laura, with a look of childish dismay; "and where shall we go for a home?"

"God will provide a home," said Mrs. Roby, very gently, having overheard the words of her little daughter. "Oh, how much need have I," she thought, "to take to myself the comfort that I would give to my children! How hard it is, in hours of anguish like these, to rest humbly, confidingly, on that eternal love which cannot but do all things well! Hath

God not said, I will never leave thee nor forsake thee? Is not his promise for ever sure: Leave thy fatherless children, I will preserve them alive; and let thy widows trust in me."

The afflicted lady was using the sword of the Spirit to repel the suggestions of mistrust and despair.

"Ah, there's the postman!" cried Aleck, starting up.

Not a word was uttered till he returned with two letters: a faint sensation came over his mother as she took them from his hand. Her children watched her anxiously as she broke the seal of the first.

"That's Mrs. Lawrence's hand," thought Aleck; "the other, written by some one whose fingers tremble very much, I am sure is from our dear old grandfather."

Bertha asked no questions, but sat with her eyes fixed upon her mother, as if waiting a sentence of life or death.

Mrs. Roby quietly read to the end of the letter, then looked upwards, and her lips slightly moved; the children thought that there was thankfulness expressed in her face. Aleck could restrain his impatience no longer. "Is there good news, mamma?" inquired he.

"Yes, very good; for I have hopes of a situation, and—"

Laura uttered an exclamation of grief. Bertha silently leaned down her head, and tried to stifle a sob.

"Is it in London?" said Aleck, looking very pale.

"In London; but this is not all; we have to thank God for mercifully taking another weight from my heart. Mrs. Lawrence, our kind, generous friend, has offered a home, in her own comfortable house, to one of my dear little girls."

Bertha looked up eagerly, Laura clapped her hands.

"To be near you, mamma, to be near you; how nice it would be! Oh! how I should like to go and live with that dear kind lady in London!"

The children anxiously watched their mother.

"One of us," murmured Bertha; "only one?" She felt her mother's loving eyes resting upon her; she dared not raise her own, for they would have overflowed. Her soul was full of an intense desire to accompany her parent to town, and be as little parted from her as possible. She feared that the wish was selfish; she would not speak more, lest she should too openly express it.

Mrs. Roby now unfolded the note from her father. Her face brightened yet more as she read the scarcely legible scrawl.

"Oh, my children!" she exclaimed, when she had finished, "how the loving care of our heavenly Friend shames our cold unthankful spirits! Here is another home opening for another child! My dear father offers a welcome to one of my daughters in his quiet peaceful dwelling at Grimlee. How can we be sufficiently thankful?"

"But which will go to London, and which to grandpapa?" cried Laura, with childish impatience.

"There is no need to decide that point directly, my love; I must think over it, before I give an answer. We must now be busy with preparations; for what I have heard this morning makes me anxious to be in London tomorrow."

"Will you take us all with you?" said Aleck, anxiety expressed in his face.

"Yes; we will remain together as long as it is possible," replied the widow, with a little tremor in her voice; "and as one of your sisters is going to Sussex, London will be all in the way." Mrs. Roby now quitted the room, to enter into the bustle of packing, arranging, making lists, paying bills, bidding a sad farewell to those amongst whom she had labored so long. Bertha assisted her as well as she could, but with a heart full almost to breaking! When her mother told her that she needed her help no longer, and sat down to her desk to answer her letters, the poor child stole with timid step to the lawn, unclosed the green gate, and passed hastily along the narrow shady lane which led to the village churchyard. In one spot, one quiet corner, where a little mound of earth appeared on which grass had not yet had time to grow, though many a flower-seed lay hidden in the sod, all Bertha's hopes and joys seemed buried. She sank on her knees by the new-made grave, and giving free vent to her distress, wept and sobbed in a passion of grief.

"Oh, papa, papa! My own precious papa," would that I could lie down and die beside you! You are gone, and now — and now — I am to be parted from my mother also!"

For Bertha had more than a suspicion on her mind that she would be the one chosen to go to Sussex, and the more the idea presented itself to her, the more intolerable she found it. She had scarcely ever seen her grandfather; affection for him there fore could not weigh in the balance against her most tender love for her mother. She thought of him only as a very old, feeble man, who had ex pressed a great dislike to the noise of children, and passed half the day dozing in his chair; who led, on small means, almost a hermit's life, in a dreary part of the country. She had heard that the widow of her uncle kept house for him at Grimlee, but of her she knew nothing at all, as Mrs. Roby herself had seen very little of her sister-in-law, and few letters had ever passed between them.

The home in London presented far greater attractions to both the little girls. The gentle manners of Mrs. Lawrence had won their hearts, while vague ideas of comfort, luxury, and pleasure always associated themselves with the image of her home. A visit to her, in happier days, had been looked for ward to with eager delight; it had been a promised pleasure which had not yet been fulfilled. But the hope of frequently meeting her mother in London was what gave intensity to Bertha's desire to be placed under the care of Mrs. Lawrence. Sussex seemed to her almost as complete a place of exile as Siberia might have been. She was a shy child, and dreaded being alone among strangers; — an affectionate daughter, and to her young heart a separation from both parents at once was like being deprived of the light of the sun; it was utter misery and desolation!

As Bertha wept in the bitterness of her spirit, she felt an arm placed gently around her, and heard a voice, which she recognized as that of her brother Aleck.

"Dear Bertha, I knew that I should find you here. This is a sad, sad time for us all."

"Sad to all, but worst, worst to me!" was her almost inarticulate reply.

"How so?" asked her brother, in some surprise.

"You at least have a home secured to you. I am like a piece of a wreck, still tossed upon the waves; there is no peace, no comfort for me!"

"You have it within!" sobbed Bertha; "you and mamma can bear up under trials; you can thank God in the midst of your troubles; you have faith, like a strong, firm anchor! But I am so different — so very different! I am so rebellious, so unthankful, so full of evil! Why, I am almost angry with poor Laura for wishing for the same thing as I do! Oh, Aleck, even you could not bear it, if you could look for a moment into my heart!"

"Dear Bertha, what do you mean?" exclaimed young Roby.

Bertha had laid her feelings under restraint in the presence of her mother, lest she should add to her sorrow; but now that restraint was removed, the floodgates were burst, and she poured forth her griefs like a torrent.

"I cannot — I cannot say. Thy will be done! I cannot be resigned to the loss of my father, or the miseries so crowding upon us! It seems to me that God has forsaken me; that he does not care what becomes of me, or how wretched and miserable I am!

I know that it is very wicked to feel in this way, and that makes me more unhappy than anything!"

The child's voice was almost choked by her sobs. "I have no faith left; no hope, no love; for I can not think that God loves me at all!"

Aleck felt shocked as well as surprised at this outburst of passion in his usually gentle, reserved little sister. He scarcely knew what to say, in order to calm her; but, taking her feverish hand in his own, he quietly pointed to a gravestone near, on which a single verse was engraven; God so loved the world, that he gave his only begotten Son, that whosoever believeth in him should not perish, hut have everlasting life. "Oh, Bertha!" said the boy, "can we look upon that, and doubt the love of our heavenly Father? He that spared not his own Son, hut delivered him up for us all, how shall he not with him also freely give us all things? I re member our dear father once saying that the blessed truth, God is love, has been signed by the hand that was pierced on the cross, and sealed in the Savior's precious blood!"

"I know it," sighed Bertha, "and I hate myself for ever doubting that love for a moment. But, when I think of leaving all that is dear, and going to Grimlee —"

"Perhaps you will not go to Grimlee," said Aleck.

17

"Oh! I'm certain that mamma will fix upon me. I saw it from her manner this morning, from some words that she dropped today."

"And does it make you doubt her love?" inquired Aleck.

"Doubt her love!" exclaimed Bertha, clasping her hands; "oh! I should die before I could doubt it! I know that she loves me — I feel it — I have proved it; she has been the best of mothers to us all!"

"And can you trust her, dear sister, and yet doubt that heavenly Father who has said, Can a woman forget her sucking child? Yea, they may forget, yet not I forget thee. I will never leave thee, nor forsake thee. I have called thee by thy name. Thou art mine!"

"Oh, Aleck, how I love you!" cried Bertha, leaning her burning brow against his shoulder, and weeping still, but less violently than before. "You help me to struggle against my evil heart!"

"I have but repeated a few texts to you, dearest, and you knew them all well before."

"Ah! but they were not in my mind; nothing good was there. I had dropped the sword of Fides: you have placed it again in my hand But oh, what shall I do without you?" she added, with a heavy sigh.

"We will think of each other, and pray for each other."

"Let us pray now — here — together, by the grave of our dear father!"

"Pray for increase of faith," murmured Aleck.

"And submission to the will of our Father in heaven!"

Aleck and his sister lingered long in the church yard. Its solemn stillness, and the exercise of devotion, gradually restored calmness to the agitated spirit of Bertha. Aleck sat beside her, with her band pressed in his; and as the quiet twilight gathered around them, in a soft, low voice, repeated to her a little hymn, which had been a favorite of their father's, and which the spot on which they rested recalled to his mind.

THE SEXTON'S HYMN

I've laid the turf above the child
Whose life was but a summer's day:
I knew that God, in mercy mild,
Had called his infant soul away.

Chorus:

Then wherefore weep
O'er those who sleep?
Their precious dust the Lord will keep.
Till he appear
In glory here.
The harvest of the world to reap.

I've laid the turf above the youth
Whose early years to God were given
Whose peaceful death proclaimed the truth
None die too soon who live for Heaven.

Chorus:

I've laid the turf o'er reverend age,
Whose hoary hairs were glory's crown:
The saint had closed his pilgrimage,
And gently laid life's burden down.

Chorus:

And soon the grave will close o'er me;
Yet wherefore mourn my life's decline?
Lord, ransomed, pardoned, saved by thee,
Sleeping or waking, I am thine!
Oh! Wherefore sigh
For those who die
In Christ? The forms that moldering lit
Shall burst the sod,
To meet their God,
And mount with seraph wings on high.

3. Generosity, and its Counterfeit

Not only by the sun is given
To yonder flowers their summer bloom;
Not only to the breeze of heaven
The roses owe their sweet perfume;

From low and earthly roots they rise,
And, born of dust, like dust must perish.
Thus with the heart's best sacrifice,
The prayers we breathe, the hopes we cherish.

Our love of good, our scorn of ill,
Earth, sordid earth, is mingled still

Mr. Probyn sat in his study, quietly reading The Times. He was a stout, comely-looking man, with a round, good-humored face, a double chin, and a smooth, shining, bald forehead. He looked like one who enjoyed the good things of life, and was well pleased that others should enjoy them; who would do a kind act, if he could do it without trouble, but who would put himself out of his way. He loved his sons, but with that selfish sort of love which considered their welfare far less than his own comfort. To watch their tempers, control their wills, form their characters and minds, was a task which he gladly left to others.

He was a kind, an indulgent parent; hut he was not one to whom his children could come for advice, or look for example. He let them have their own way, follow their own course, with an easy assurance that their hearts were good, and all would be right in the end. The Bible truth, that the heart is deceitful, and desperately wicked, Mr. Probyn had never really believed. He had no doubt but that all was right within, as long as no crime was committed that could come under the notice of the police, or incur the censure of the world. Surrounded by the misery which abounds in a great city, he had a comfortable persuasion that the world was going on well

21

enough.

He knew not, cared not, how others might live, as long as his own table was luxuriously supplied. Soul, take thine ease; eat, drink, and he merry. Such was the motto of his life. He wronged no man, hated no man, could give liberally from his abundance that which he never missed. This, he thought, comprised all his duty towards his neighbor; and as for his duty towards his God, his conscience never troubled him about that.

"Well, my boy, what do you want?" said Mr. Probyn, raising his spectacled eyes from his paper, as Constantine entered the room.

"Papa I have a favor to ask of you."

"I daresay, I daresay," laughed his father. "Man wants but little here below, says the poet; but he knew very little of boys."

"Next Tuesday is our birthday, papa." "When you are as old as I, Con, you'll not care to remember your birthdays; they come round a great deal too fast, ha, ha, ha! But I suppose that you come to remind me of your watch."

With rather a hesitating manner Constantine, approached, and laid his hand on the back of Mr. Probyn's armchair.

"Would you object, papa, to give me, instead of the watch, the money which it would cost you?"

"Heigho!" exclaimed Mr. Probyn, in some surprise; "going to begin making a fortune already? I should like to know what a young fellow like you would think of doing with ten pounds!"

"You know that Mr. Roby, our tutor, died lately: he has left his widow very poor."

"Sony for that; he should have laid by. It's astonishing to see the improvidence of some people," said the rich man, who had never known a want. "I have heard something," said Constantine. "of Mrs., Roby having lost in a bank some money that had been settled upon her. Besides, all the people about Dove's Nest were so poor, that their clergy man —"

"Thought that he must keep them in countenance, ha, ha, ha!"

"I should much like to be allowed to send that ten pounds to Mrs. Roby," said Constantine, coming to the point.

Here the conversation was interrupted by the entrance of a stranger upon business, as the powdered servant announced Mr. Gruffly, and a short, ill proportioned figure entered, with an awkward, swinging gait, which accorded with the rough, weather-beaten features of a face whose characteristic was frank good humor.

Mr. Gruffly was partner in a large shipping concern, and far better accustomed to business than to society, as might be seen from the manner in which he seated himself on the velvet-cushioned chair which the servant had placed for his accommodation.

"I was in this quarter, to speak to one of our captains," said he, resting one of his broad hands on each knee, "or I would not have troubled you so early. If you're engaged just now with the young gentleman, why, my business is not like time and tide — it can wait till his is knocked off."

"Well, Gruffly, what would you say to a boy who, instead of a gold watch, wanted ten pounds to send to the widow of his tutor?"

"Say! I'd say he was a fine little fellow; and I'd clap another ten at the top of 'em."

Neither Constantine nor his father could help laughing at the hint; Gruffly himself laughed loudest of the three. "And who was this tutor of yours, my man?" said he, clapping Constantine on the shoulder. "He must have been an uncommon sort of master; for boys are not generally over-fond of those who flog the Latin grammar into 'em."

"Mr. Roby, the clergyman —"

"What! Alexander Roby, the admiral's son, my old school-fellow!" exclaimed the rough but kind- hearted man, " I heard of his death, poor fellow, but didn't know that he'd left a widow behind And she's poor, is she?" he added, with interest.

"Very poor," was the answer of Constantine.

"Are there children?"

"Yes; three."

"Any boys?"

"One boy, who is older than myself."

"I wonder if we couldn't make something of him," said Gruffly, passing his hand through his shock of rough hair, as was his manner when turning over some thought in his mind,

"We might put him as a middy aboard one of our ships, and say nothing about the fee, d'ye see? We want some smart young fellows for our Indiamen, and 'twould take him off his poor mother's hands. Would you oblige me with her address?"

So frankly, so simply did Gruffly make his proposition, that Constantine had hardly an idea that he intended to confer any favor at all upon the widow. Little aware was either he or his father that the fee which Gruffly seemed scarcely to think worth mentioning would be sixty pounds, taken from his own pocket.

There are some to whom conferring kindnesses seems to come as naturally, and without effort, as for a fountain to throw up its waters. Happy such, when generosity arises from a holy principle within; every drop shall catch the sunlight of heaven — every drop shall return to them in blessings! There is that scattereth, and yet increasethIt is more blessed to give than to receive.

Constantine repeated the address of Mrs. Roby very willingly, though with a secret doubt on his mind that the ship owner's offer would be at all acceptable to his late companion. Aleck had never had a fancy for the sea. Studious and clever, he was formed to distinguish himself in the paths of literature, and he knew it; and though by no means deficient in courage, the rough, perilous life of a seaman presented few charms for him.

Mr. Probyn, who did not choose to appear back ward when benevolence was the order of the day, opened his desk, and, in a manner which seemed to say, "I'm doing a very liberal thing," handed over twenty pounds in notes to his son; while Gruffly, unclasping a huge pocketbook, crammed full of papers, carefully took down the address of Mrs. Roby.

GENEROSITY.

Few good deeds bear close examination, so mingled are our motives, so tainted our best works with the evil belonging to our nature. Let Constantine, therefore, as with eager pleasure he encloses the banknotes to his afflicted friend, be thought by us, what he thinks himself, a generous, kindhearted and grateful boy. Perhaps the beggar girl, who shares her crust with a child yet poorer than her self, is more generous, for to her the sacrifice is greater, as her need is more pressing.

Perhaps Constantine has a secret consciousness that he will not be very long suffered to want even the watch which he has offered to give up; perhaps a little desire of approbation has strengthened his resolution to do a generous act; perhaps (but this he never suspects himself) his pride is gratified at his being able to patronize those to whom he has hitherto been obliged to look up. He makes an unconscious balance in his mind between Aleck's superior talents and his own greater wealth, and feels himself placed above young Roby, by the very fact that he can offer him assistance.

Mr. Probyn, his son, and Mr. Gruffly, had each performed a liberal deed, to relieve the same case of distress. In the eyes of man their merit might be the same, but not in the sight of Heaven,

Gruffly had acted from feelings of benevolence and friendship, warming into stronger action, but not taking the place of a constant high sense of duty. He would have helped a widow had her husband never been his friend — nay, even had he been his enemy, and have neither wished for human praise, nor thought that his action merited it.

Constantine's motives, as we have seen, were mixed; yet, from one brought up in selfish indulgence, the act was full of promise. It was an onward step in the narrow path; it was a good blow struck at selfishness within; it was doubtless pleasing to Him who despiseth not the day of small things. But Mr. Probyn had bestowed his liberal donation not from love of God, or pity for the afflicted. It was easier to give than to refuse. He liked to have the character of a generous, kindhearted man. As he was wealthy, it could be purchased without loss of anything that the selfish man prized. But this is not the giving which is blessed. These are not 'the alms which, like those of Cornelius, rise as a memorial above.

Charlotte Maria Tucker

4. Poverty and Pride

Some crosses are from Heaven sent,
And some we fashion of our own;

By envy, pride, and discontent,
What thorns upon our path are strewn?

Not these the thorns that form the crown,
Not such the cross that lifts on high;

Our sharpest trials we lay down.
When sin and self we crucify.

I would speak to you a little, my Bertha," said the gentle voice of Mrs. Roby, as she entered that evening the small room where her daughter was engaged in packing her box.

"Dear mamma, pray sit down." Bertha placed a chair, and then seated herself down at the feet of her mother, resting her arms upon the widow's knee.

"I have been thinking over the letters which we received this morning, and praying to be directed my child. As Laura is so young, and therefore re quires such watchful care, it seems to me" — Mrs. Roby paused, she was fearful of giving pain — "it seems to me to be best that the little one should be placed in a home near me."

"It is best," replied Bertha, in a low voice.

"And you, my thoughtful, attentive child, will be a comfort to my dear aged father. I feel that I am sending to him one in whom he will find a blessing, not a burden."

Bertha kissed her mother's hand, and was silent.

"I cannot tell you what a relief it is to me that this arrangement does not disappoint you, that you see the reasons for it, and acquiesce so readily, dear Bertha."

"I do not say," replied Bertha, forcing a smile, though a bright drop quivered on her lashes, "that I should not have preferred remaining nearer you; but I am sure that your decision is good, and I will try — to be all that you think me to grandpapa."

Mrs. Roby pressed her daughter to her heart in a very long, a very close embrace; and, in the feeling that she had pleased and comforted her mother, the poor child was almost repaid for the effort which her calmness had cost her.

"You must now, Bertha, as you will be separated from your early guides, learn to think more, and act more for yourself. Your grandfather must be burdened with no cares, and I would not have you give trouble to your aunt; yet would I be very unwilling that your education should be entirely neglected, that you should forget all that I have taught you when my eye is over you no more."

"Shall I go on with my lessons by myself?"

"Two hours every day I should wish you to devote to improving your mind and pursuing your studies. I need not remind you that the one thing needful should ever have the first place in your attention, the first claim on your time. Your Bible, your prayer, your hymn of praise, let nothing ever lead you to neglect. To come to minor things, my Bertha, it seems to me that, under the circumstances in which you will be placed, you should yourself take charge of your wardrobe. I will supply you with an allowance for necessaries, two pounds a quarter —"

"Oh, mamma, that is a great deal too much!" cried Bertha.

"I do not think that you could manage upon less; if you find the sum insufficient, write to me frankly for more. My salary, should I be with Lady Bunnington, will enable me, I trust, to supply you."

"But if I should not spend so much?" inquired Bertha.

"Oh, anything that you can save, you may have for yourself — consider it entirely as your own."

What trifles serve to distress or please the mind of a child! To Bertha eight pounds a-year seemed an inexhaustible sum, and she was gratified more than she could express by being intrusted with so much. Her busy little brain was now not only full of plans of economy and retrenchment, but she actually began to arrange in what way she would spend her accumulated savings — how her mother was to be surprised with the unexpected arrival of something which she needed but would not purchase, or Aleck be helped on in his struggle for a livelihood by the willing self-denial of his sister?

These thoughts made Bertha look so much more cheerful and hopeful than her brother had expected that evening to see her, that he was at a loss to comprehend the cause of her composure. The painful day closed peacefully over the afflicted inmates of Dove's Nest; and the mother, as she retired at length to sleep for the last time under the roof where her happiest years had been passed, thanked God humbly and heartily for the mercies which had so sweetened her bitter cup of affliction.

She awoke, however, the next morning with an almost intolerable burden on her heart. The day had arrived on which she was to quit home, friends, and — saddest of all — the grave where slept the re mains of him whom she had loved best upon earth. Every object on which the eye of the widow rested gave her an additional pang, while her approaching parting with Bertha and Aleck, and the uncertainty which hung over her boy's future fate, oppressed her with a crushing weight of care. Cast thy burden on the Lord, he will sustain thee, the poor lady murmured over and over to herself, as she commenced the duties of the day. She could scarcely return the greeting of her children, scarcely command her voice through the morning prayer; and yet from that prayer she arose refreshed, strengthened for the painful trial before her.

When the postman came on his accustomed round, she saw him herself, to bid a kind farewell to one whom she had known for years. The man left the door brushing away a tear with the back of his rough hand, and wishing with all his soul that the letters which he had brought might convey some tidings of comfort to the widow lady.

As on the former morning, there were two, both of them addressed to Mrs., Roby. She flushed as she perused the first, and, without a single word of comment, handed it across the table to Aleck. Bertha saw that his color mounted also, but he looked rather surprised and agitated than pleased

"May I show the letter to Bertha, mamma?"

Mrs. Roby bowed assent, but still spoke not Aleck passed his hand across his brow.

"It is an opening for me, certainly," he said, al most as if speaking to himself; "but I had never thought of going to sea."

"I leave you free in this matter to decide for yourself, my own dear boy," said Mrs. Roby. "You know everything connected with our circumstances; I will not attempt to influence you in a matter on which the welfare of your whole life may depend."

"I long to be independent; but the sea —"

"Is Aleck going to be a sailor?" exclaimed little Laura — "to go on the deep, deep sea, and visit all sorts of strange countries, and bring home all kinds of beautiful things, and get a rich man, and take care of mamma! Oh, how I wish that I were a boy! I would sail away with him too!"

There was something cheering in the tone of the little girl's voice and the animated glance of her eye. It was well that one of the party could see sunshine where to the rest all was mist and gloom. Occupied with her anxious thoughts, scarcely giving attention to what she was doing, Mrs. Roby opened the second letter, which, as our reader may have guessed, was from Constantine. Her astonishment, and that of her children, may be imagined, when from it fell several bank-notes. The widow gazed upon the money as Elijah might have gazed on the food which the ravens brought to him in the wilderness.

"Lord, this is from thee!" was the language of her heart.

Constantine's note was now eagerly perused. The little girls had no feeling but that of gratitude and pleasure. Laura exclaimed that the "bad, bad boy," as she had once called him, had grown to be worth his weight in gold! Bertha wonderingly remembered the time when she would as soon have expected kindness from a wolf or a bear, as generosity and tenderness from Constantine Probyn. But Mrs. Roby still looked pensive and thoughtful, letting the banknotes lie untouched before her, while Aleck compressed his lips and knit his brow, as if the sight of them gave pain instead of pleasure.

"Is not Con a dear, kind boy!" cried little Laura

"Well enough," replied Aleck, almost testily.

"Surely we should be grateful to him, Aleck," said Bertha, surprised at the manner of her brother. "Does he not say that he gave up his gold watch?"

"Why should he say anything about it?" exclaimed Aleck. "We never begged or borrowed from him. My mother is not one to have money flung at her!"

"Oh, Aleck!" exclaimed both his sisters at once.

"I hope that you will send it back at once, mamma," said the boy, pushing his chair back from the table; "I can't bear that you should be indebted to Con for this money."

"I shall accept it very gratefully as a loan, which, if I obtain employment, I shall hope to repay within the year. If you go to sea, I shall need it for your outfit — if you remain, for your support in England. This relieves me from a burden of care."

"I am sure that Constantine meant to be very kind," said Bertha, who did not understand the cause of the emotion of her brother. But Mrs. Roby read more deeply into his heart.

She saw in the letter of Constantine touches of the pride and self satisfaction which had robbed his generosity of half its grace; and she saw in the countenance of her son the same pride, rising against the idea of obligation towards one on whom he had secretly looked down. Pride tempts not the rich alone — he has his galling chain for the poor. It is hard so to confer a great favor, that Pride shall not dim the luster of the gift, by leaving the mark of his touch upon it; harder still to receive it with gratitude and meek ness, and treasure up the remembrance of the benefit. Pride chills benevolence and stifles gratitude; makes the giver unlovable, the receiver unloving.

Oh, how, in the current of daily life, unnoticed, unsuspected, yet embittering all, mingles the poison of that unholy root which has been planted by the hand of Pride!

I will not dwell long upon the melancholy departure from Dove's Nest. I will not describe the last hurried, tearful look at every room, endeared by association; nor say how Bertha and Laura, with glistening eyes, plucked roses from every favorite bush, to bear away — poor fading memorials of happier days. The note of the cuckoo seemed, to their ears, to breathe farewell; the villagers formed a line at the gate, weeping, and blessing her who had watched over their welfare so long Scarcely had the carriage left them behind, when the eyes of the afflicted widow and her children instinctively turned towards the tower of the church, and watched it as long as it remained in sight, till a heavy sigh broke from every heart as the trees hid it from view.

The journey to the railway was a very silent one; low sobs from the little girls, and a few words of comfort from their agitated mother, in whose fond arms they were infolded, were all that passed before they reached the station.

There was then a brief period of bustle, in which Aleck made himself actively useful to his mother; but when all had taken their seats in a second-class carriage, and the shrill whistle gave its signal for motion, he drew his cap down lower over his eyes, and uttered not a single word till his journey was concluded. There was much passing in the mind of the boy as the train rattled noisily on — a reviewing of old, long cherished hopes. He had not known how dear they were till now, when the hour appeared come for dashing them all to the ground! Aleck, in the secret depths of his heart, had resolved to be a great, a distinguished man — to gain money by his talents, and expend it in beneficence — to do good, and win the gratitude of many.

He had built up a fairy fabric, and now it was crumbling into dust! Instead of helping others, he himself required help; instead of conferring obligations, he was obliged to receive them. And what availed it him that he had been esteemed advanced in his studies far beyond his years? Would it soften the hardships of a rough sea-life, earn him distinction on his mid night watch, or enable him to mount the rigging with more ease and safety in a storm?

Aleck considered himself though he could not have given a shape to the thought in words, thrown away if he accepted Gruffly's offer. Why not decline it, then, and climb to distinction in some way more congenial to his taste? Aleck had prayed for the means of independence, and this sudden opening seemed like an answer to prayer. He knew no other way by which he could relieve his mother from the burden of his support. God had chosen for him, and should he murmur because the Almighty's ways are not as our ways! The more Aleck reflected on the subject, the clearer appeared the path of duty. It was painful, but what of that!

He looked at his sister Bertha. She had wiped away her tears; she was struggling now to look cheerful. She was listening kindly to the prattle of little Laura, though it turned on the rather unfortunate subject of the pleasure of going to Mrs. Lawrence. She was showing every attention to her mother which the tenderest consideration could suggest. No one knew better than Aleck what the sufferings of his sister had been. He had comforted and supported her by his words; and now, in his time of difficulty, her example com forted and supported him.

"After all," considered the boy, as a deep sigh followed his silent resolution to enter the profession which he disliked — "after all, the things which art seen are temporal; this is a passing, changing scene. When once we arrive at the heavenly shore, we shall care little if we reached it through storm or calm. There will be no more trial, or parting, or poverty there; and the things which are not seen are eternal"

Charlotte Maria Tucker

5. Dark Clouds and Blue Sky

One friend was ere near,
Soothing and blessing;
What could the Christian fear.
Such love possessing!

The streets of London looked glistening and brown, the carriage wheels left a deep track in the mud, from the leaden sky dropped the drizzling rain, when, three days after the arrival of the family in the great city, a party stood on the platform beside a long railway train, which was now about to start. It consisted of a lady in deep mourning, accompanied by two boys, who had just placed in one of the carriages a pale and agitated child,

"Pray, pray do not wait here, dearest mamma!" said Bertha, leaning forward from the window; "you will be Bo wet with the rain! You will write to me soon, will you not? And let me know, dear Aleck, when you are to sail for India." The tremulous voice could not utter more; but what love was expressed in the long gaze of the tearful eyes and the grasp of the cold little hand!

"Goodbye, my precious child! God go with you!"

"Goodbye, Bertha!" cried Constantine cheer fully, taking off his hat as the train began slowly to move. Aleck ran by the side, to keep his eyes as long as possible on that dear little face, which he might not for many months see again.

"I say, my little lady, you must not lean out so," said a rough but good-humored voice from the in side of the carriage. "We'll have another train passing, and whisking off your head, and what will you do without that?"

Bertha sank back on her seat, weeping.

"Don't cry so, my good child," said the same voice; " but bear up, like a brave little girl. I daresay now that you are going to school, and don't like the idea of sky-blue milk, and cold dripping in stead of butter."

"No, sir," replied Bertha timidly; "I am going to be with my grandfather."

"Going to your grandfather, eh? A savage old gentleman, I suppose, with a stout crabstick, which he is pretty fond of laying over your shoulders?"

"Oh no, sir!" exclaimed Bertha, unable to help smiling in the midst of her tears.

"Well, then, I don't see why you should get up the waterworks like that: don't you think we've enough of that sort of thing already?" he added, as he put up the window to keep out the rain."

Bertha ventured to glance up for a moment, and met the frank, kindly look of an elderly man, rather stout in person, and somewhat shabbily dressed, who occupied the seat just opposite to her.

"There, let me stick your umbrella into the netting for you; you'll want it at the end of your journey," pursued her companion; "and make a footstool of my little black box. Who were those who came to see you off? I thought that I recognized the face of one of the young fellows, but I can't just remember where I met him."

"The tall one was—"

"No, no; I don't mean him with the lank, light hair, but the one who was waving his cap."

"His name is Constantine Probyn."

"Ah! that's it!" cried the traveler, slapping his knee; "I thought that I'd seen him before! I should not wonder, then, if the widow lady were Mrs. Roby herself."

"Yes, yes; it was my mother," said Bertha.

"So you're the child of my poor old school-fellow said he, in whom my reader has doubtless recognized Mr. Gruffly; " and that tall boy was your brother, I suppose, who is to sail as middy in the Mermaid?"

"Yes; it was Aleck," said Bertha, a little proudly.

"I should not say, by the cut of his jib, that nature had meant him for a sailor. But I daresay that he'll do very well, and that we shall make a man of him yet."

Bertha perceived that her bluff companion was in some way connected with the sea, and concerned in her brother's appointment. Mustering up her courage — for though Gruffly's voice was rather loud, there was something in his manner which inspired confidence — she ventured to ask for information on a subject on which her mind had been painfully dwelling.

"Is the sea very dangerous, sir?"

Mr. Gruffly leaned back and laughed. "Old Shakespeare says, my little maid, 'It's dangerous to eat, to drink, to sleep; ' have you never heard the sailors' song: —

'Foolhardy chaps that live on shore,
What dangers they are all in!
For they lie quaking in their beds
For fear the roof should fall in!'

"But," he added, gravely, resting his hands on his knees, and leaning forward, "your father's daughter need not be told that there is the same care over us on sea as on land, and that those who trust in that watchful care need fear no evil wherever they go."

"I like him," thought Bertha to herself. "He has a very kind face, though so brown and rough; and I should think that he must be a good man."

"And so you're going to your grandfather," resumed Mr. Gruffly, after an interval of silence; "I suspect with a purse a little lighter than your heart." He was searching in his large pocket for something, and Bertha, who suspected his intention, flushed crimson up to her very temples.

"I have a great deal of money," she said hurriedly, when he had drawn out and unclasped a leathern pocket-book, and selected the brightest sovereign which it contained, with an evident design of transferring it to her.

Mr. Gruffly's Generosity.

"Hey!" said he rather surprised; "pray what do you call a great deal?"

"A whole pound in gold and another in silver."

"Two pounds, my little Croesus! Well, here's another to keep them company: —

Multiplication
Is no vexation,
Addition is not bad;
Sovereigns three
Won't puzzle thee,
Nor their jingle drive thee mad.

Gruffly laughed heartily at his own joke, and pressed the gold on Bertha; but, with the feelings of a lady, she shrank back from receiving it.

"Mamma might not like me to — indeed you are very, very kind — but — "

"Not a word more about the matter," said Gruffly in the tone of one who would take no denial. "Here we are at my station already; I wish you a good journey, my child. Keep a brave heart, and remember there's blue sky behind the thickest cloud. God bless you!"

The next moment he was gone.

"How very generous and kind he was," thought Bertha. "I wish that I had had presence of mind to thank him; but I felt so much surprised, and confused, and perplexed. I will write and tell mamma all about it. He evidently knew my dear father; he spoke of being his school-fellow. I wonder who he can be! Perhaps Mr. Gruffly who gave Aleck the appointment. Oh, how stupid I was not to think of that before! — How ungrateful not to thank him for his goodness!"

On, on again rushed the puffing engine and train, but the heart of little Bertha felt lighter, though every mile passed was taking her farther from those whom she loved. She had been cheered by the kindness of one whom she had never met before and might never meet again. He had thrown a ray of brightness upon a gloomy path, and had not lost the opportunity afforded by a short journey on a railway to speak the word in season which had been balm to a bleeding spirit. "I will fear no evil," thought Bertha, "but keep a brave heart, and look for the blue sky behind the black cloud. There may be good days in store for us yet"

Different passengers entered and quitted the carriage at various stations, but none took any further notice of Bertha. She sat very still, busied with her own thoughts, too shy to open the little packet of refreshments which her thoughtful mother had provided for her comfort. The poor child, un accustomed to travel alone, began to be perplexed by various petty fears. She knew the name of the station at which she was to stop; but what if she should pass it without knowing, and be carried off whither she knew not! Every time that the train stopped she was nervously anxious till she could see the name of the station, for she was too timid to ask for information, either from the passengers or the guard. Then she wondered to herself again and again how, amidst the quantity of trunks which she had seen stowed in the luggage van, she should ever find out the wooden box which contained all that she had in the world.

This was to her an absolute mountain of difficulty, which she felt almost hopeless of surmounting; and beyond it appeared another — how she should, when she left the train, make her way to her grandfather's house. True, her aunt knew that she was coming, and had promised to send some one to meet her, but the fear that this "some one " would not have arrived, or if arrived, would not find her out, greatly disturbed the mind of the child.

At length Bertha thought that she heard the name of the right station called out by the guard, though his quick, short utterance rendered her doubtful He came near her, and repeated the word. This time she was sure that she was right, and leaning forward, made a timid effort to draw his attention to her. In another minute the door of the carriage was flung open by him, and she sprang hurriedly down the steep step upon the plat form, too eager, in her haste lest the train should move on, and too anxious about the fate of her box, to notice that both umbrella and packet of sandwiches were left behind!

About the box her mind was speedily relieved. The station was a small and very quiet one, no passenger but herself was stopping there, and she saw her property, with her mother's neatly directed card upon it, safely deposited on the wet, glistening platform. Bertha, freed from two of her troubles, was now to encounter the third. She looked un easily round for some one who might be on the watch for her arrival She saw no one but the railway official, who had evidently nothing to do with her; and as she stood in the rain beside the box which she feared to leave, glancing nervously in every direction to see any face that wore the look of a friend, the poor fatherless girl felt a sensation of terrible desolation. The train by which she had come was now again in motion; she watched it rushing away, becoming smaller and smaller in the distance, with its light cloud of steam rolling above it; and there was she left, friendless and alone! Truly the sky was very dark above her.

"Are you expecting some one, miss?" said the official. His voice almost startled the little girl, yet gave her a feeling of hope.

"Yes; is any person waiting to receive me?" she replied. He looked around and shook his head.

"Can you show me then, sir, the road to Mr. Chipstone's?" said Bertha, with a desperate idea in her mind of finding out the way to her grandfather's by herself

"Chipstone? — I don't know the name, — I've come here but lately," answered the man, civilly. "I'm sorry that I cannot help you. But had you not better remain a Utile while in the waiting- room, miss, and not stop out in the rain?"

Poor Bertha had hardly been aware that it was raining, and now first missed her umbrella. It was no small loss to one so poor, and she was much annoyed at her own carelessness, as well as inconvenienced by its effects. As she stood with an expression of doubt and distress on her young face which moved the pity of the man at the station, a rough-looking ploughman, in smock-frock and straw hat, sauntered on the platform and addressed him with the words, "I say, has a box or trunk been left here with the name of Roby upon it?"

The official pointed to Bertha's, and said, "That belongs to the young lady here."

"I'se sent by Missus Chipstone to bring it, and show miss the way to the house;" and so saying, he stooped down and heaved up the box on his broad shoulder.

"Have you not brought a fly? It is raining," said the other, watching the plashing drops as they fell

"I'se no orders but to bring the box and the child, I guess as neither will melt by the way."

"No, no, I would not have a fly, I can easily walk, it does not rain much," cried poor Bertha, whose anxiety to save for her widowed mother made her grudge any unnecessary expense

She set out on her walk with her rough guide The man at the station long watched her little form, as she pursued her way along a narrow country road, and an exclamation of pity broke from his lips; for her mourning, her pale face, her apparent friendlessness, told even to a stranger a tide of woe.

The way seemed terribly long, all the more so as the road was heavy from rain, and the little girl could sometimes scarcely pick her way, or lift her feet from the thick miry clay which clogged her shoes as she toiled painfully along. Now, too, she began to feel faint from hunger, for she had scarcely been able to touch her breakfast, and glad indeed would she have been of the provisions which she had left behind her in the train. "But I'll soon be at home," thought the poor child, Alas! even home did not now appear to her eyes in the bright coloring of hope, so unpromising seemed her reception at the station, so damped were her spirits by fatigue, hunger, and the trials which her feelings had undergone.

Yet there was still one source of pure consolation open to the fatherless Bertha, — one strong support to the trembling heart, to which it now clung more closely than ever. She dwelt on the words of the stranger whom she had met in the railway carriage. "Fear no evil," she repeated to herself; and why should I fear no evil? For Thou art with me — the Lord is with me. He who knew what it was to be sad, hungry, and faint, who met unkindness where he looked for love; he if with me still, will be with me always. Oh, what a blessed thing it is to know that nothing can separate me from him!"

At length the weary child arrived at the small, lonely dwelling which was to be her future abode. In former days it perhaps had been pretty, for large trees had shaded it then, which had lately been cut down and sold as timber; and lovely flowers had then bloomed in the garden, which now held only cabbages and potatoes. Green weeds were growing on the gravel walk; the windows of the house were dimmed with dust, and their curtains looked patched and dingy. The whole appearance of the place matched the gloomy aspect of the weather.

Bertha timidly knocked at the entrance. "Come in, the door is not locked," cried a voice from with in; and a hard-featured woman, with a cold, dry manner, came out from the parlor to meet her.

"So, here you are, all dripping and drowned." How had your mother the folly not to give you an umbrella?"

"She gave me one," said Bertha, "but unfortunately I forgot it, and left it in the train"

"Stupid child," muttered Mrs. Chipstone to herself. "Take up that box to the little back room, will you?" she said, addressing the ploughman; "and scrape your shoes before you go up the stairs."

"May I go and see grandpapa?" inquired Bertha, looking towards the parlor with a yearning for one kind word of welcome from some one.

"Thoughtless child, you would give him his death of cold, like a drowned mouse as you are! I sup pose," she added, after a minute's consideration, "that your mother did not forget to give you some thing to eat on your journey?"

"Oh no, she provided me with sandwiches; but — "

"Then you'll wait very well till teatime at seven," said Mrs. Chipstone, abruptly closing the conversation. "Go and unpack your box, and dry your clothes, and give the man a shilling for his trouble."

Bertha crept quietly up the creaking stair to the little, musty, scarcely furnished room, which she was henceforth to call her own. There was no blind to the window, nor press beside the wall; her own box must serve her for table and chair; the spider had stretched her thick web above the bed, and dust formed the only carpet.

The man had just finished uncording the box

Bertha timidly offered him a shilling. He took it, looked at it, began to grumble, she instantly put another into his hand. Poor as she was, Mrs. Roby had taught her daughter always to give the laborer the fair price for his work, nor stoop to the mean ness, of which even the rich are sometimes guilty, of underpaying those who serve them.

The first thing which Bertha did when she found herself alone, was to kneel down, and in an earnest, agitated prayer, commended herself to the orphan's God. She then obeyed the order of her aunt, and felt the comfort of being again clad in dry garments. She drew out her little desk, and began a long, loving letter to her mother, dwelling a good deal upon the kindness of Mr. Gruffly, but not mentioning the opposite conduct of her aunt. She found it hard to avoid crying as she wrote, she so pined for one look of her mother again, one kind word from Aleck, one bright smile from her dear little sister! Leaving her note unfinished, that it might contain an account of her meeting with her grandfather, Bertha descended the staircase, and entering the parlor, to her great relief found him there alone.

The poor old man had become almost too feeble to rise from his seat. Illness had affected his speech, and he could hardly express himself distinctly. But the frost of age had not chilled the warmth of his heart, and he gave his poor little grandchild such an affectionate welcome, stroking her pale cheek, pressing her to him, and calling her by tender, loving names, that Bertha could no longer restrain her tears, and they flowed freely, but silently, on his bosom. She was startled by the entrance of her aunt

"Absurd nonsense! Folly and affectation! We want no crying babies here!" The orphan's tears were dried in a moment. Her grandfather looked sympathizing and kind, but neither on this occasion nor on any other did he venture to oppose the imperious woman who ruled his house with a rod of iron.

He was too old and feeble for anything but submission, and was treated in his own home like a child.

"Will tea-time never arrive!" thought Bertha She was almost fainting with hunger and fatigue, and the weary hours seemed as though they never would end. At length the family sat down to a meal so scanty that a child with a moderate appetite could easily have consumed all that was placed upon the table. Bertha, who was of a shy and retiring disposition, scarcely ventured to help herself to any thing, with the cold eye of that hard woman upon her. Hungry she sat down, hungry she arose, hungry she went to her little chamber at night — there, at least, she could cry unmolested. But when at length, stretched on her small hard bed, the poor orphan's eyes closed in slumber, Heaven sent her sweet dreams of peace and joy. She thought herself again in her own dear home, with her mother sitting be side her. The Bible lay open on her knee, and she was reading from the beautiful psalm of David, I will fear no evil, for Thou art with me.

Then she saw a bright light fall on the page, but not like the light of the sun, and heard a soft sound, as of whistling wings; and as she glanced upwards, she marveled to see a ray of glory streaming from above; and beautiful beings came glancing in that ray, with sparkling crowns and wreaths of colored flame; and she knew one dear face which she had fondly loved, which wore a smile of rapture and love, such as mortal never wore upon earth!" "Who are these?" she seemed to murmur in her sleep; and a voice like an angel's replied these are they which came out of great tribulation. They shall hunger no more, nor thirst any more, and God shall wipe away all tears from their eyes.

So peacefully slept the weary child, with dreams such as a monarch might have envied. In her comfortless chamber in that dreary place she might yet say with Jacob, when he arose from his grassy couch and stony pillow, surely the Lord is in this; place. This is none other hut the house of God, and this is the gate of heaven.

6. Toil And Trial.

Ah! why take thought for those whose God is near?
For those whom Christ will comfort, wherefore fear?

Were the whole earth, on which the watery bow
Appears to rest, involved in overthrow,
Its bright arch would not sink, nor one soft tint forego!

Safe may we leave them to their God alone,
To him whose tender love exceeds our own.

Idly Mrs. Roby turned from the station whence she had watched the departure of her child. She seemed still to feel the pressure of the little hand, and to see the loving, earnest eyes bent upon her. But this was the time for action, not for regret; there was much to be done and small space in which to do it, for on that day she was to enter upon her new situation, and Aleck's outfit was yet to be procured.

"What's to be your next piece of business?" said Constantine.

"We must go to the outfitter's, and thence to the docks. I must see and personally thank Mr. Gruffly. This is the last opportunity that I may have." "Shall we stop another cab, then?" said the boy. "You can't go wandering about in the rain. Aleck will have enough of the water, I should think, with out trying a cold shower-bath here."

"Not a cab; we will stop the first omnibus going in the direction which we must take."

"An omnibus!" exclaimed Con, with great con tempt; "am I going in such a vehicle as that I should be ashamed for any one to see me."

"There should be no shame except where there is a sin."

"But it is not proper for a lady."

"It is proper for a lady, as far as it is possible, to suit her expenses to her means. I am already too deeply indebted to my friends to —"

"Oh, pray don't speak about that," exclaimed Constantine; and Aleck, to whom the conversation was extremely unpleasant, put a stop to it by hailing an omnibus.

"Good-bye," said young Probyn, as they parted, "Aleck, I could half wish myself in your shoes; it would be glorious fun going to sea!"

Aleck looked as if he were of quite a different opinion. Con returned homewards, in a meditative mood.

"Well, after all," he reflected, "I think that Mrs. Roby is right. It is meaner to spend the money of other people in procuring indulgences for ourselves, than; it would be to ride even in a cart! I remember hearing of a lady who kept her carriage, and dressed in the height of the fashion, and died thousands of pounds in debt to her tradesmen! That's what I should call dishonesty: ay and treachery too; for they trusted her, and she deceived them. It was a kind of hypocrisy besides, making believe that she was rich when she was poor. Dishonesty, treachery, hypocrisy! Yes; these are the things which are not proper for a lady!"

Constantine was met at his own home by Adolphus, in a state of joyful excitement.

"Hurrah! Hurrah! I've got my watch! Such a beauty! Is it not a splendid one Con?"

Con was not magnanimous enough to take much pleasure in admiring his brother's birthday gift. He, however, said that it seemed a very nice one.

"Now, are you not vexed that you have nothing yourself?"

"I have something," said Constantine quietly; "something better, perhaps, that even a watch."

"I would not exchange with you," said Adolphus laughing; "I like something solid, my good fellow!"

If solidity he estimated by duration, how light and flimsy is any mere pleasure of time, compared to that which extends to eternity! The one is as the sparkle of the short-lived firefly, the other as the bright stars of heaven!

Mrs. Roby found Mr. Gruffly absent from his home, as my readers are aware. She then proceeded to execute her business. She felt deeply sad, as she completed the preparations for the departure of her only son. Aleck assumed a liveliness of manner, admired the comfortable dark blue Jersey, in which he should bid defiance to the weather, and donned his gold-laced cap with an air of cheerfulness which belied the feelings of his heart. He returned with his mother to Mrs. Lawrence's house, in which he was to remain till he sailed; and after Mrs. Roby had there bidden farewell to her friend, and her little Laura, he escorted his mother to Grosvenor Place, where she was to enter on her situation as governess,

"If I do not see you again before you start, my own boy, remember;" the mother's voice failed her, and she leaned more heavily on the arm of her son.

"Oh, mother, Laura and I will come and see you every day!"

"No, no; that cannot be — I shall not be in my own home; I shall have no right to bring my children into the dwelling of another."

"You will come and see us, then?"

"My time is not my own; I must devote it to the fulfillment of my duties."

"But you are no slave to these people," cried Aleck, proudly.

"Not their slave, my son, but God's servant. My obligations towards them must be fulfilled as to Him. I am bound to devote all my energies to their service."

"Oh, mother, mother, this is what I cannot bear! I could endure anything myself; but not that you should lose home, comforts, your very liberty of action — that you should sell your time and your strength to strangers!"

"Nay," replied Mrs. Roby, gently; "shall I not rather be thankful that I have been granted that time and strength, and given opportunity to use them for the benefit of my children; and that I am still permitted to work for my Lord — to feed his lambs, when parted from my own!"

As she spoke, she laid her hand on a door-bell, for by this time they had arrived in Grosvenor Place. A few whispered words, an earnest grasp, and the mother and son had parted! What an aching void remained in the heart of each!

Lady Bunnington was out driving in her carriage; the governess was at once ushered into the school room, her future post of duty, the sphere of her arduous but most important functions. The apartment was occupied by the young ladies of the family, who, to judge from the loud voices and merry laughter which met Mrs. Roby's ear before she entered, were certainly not busy with their studies.

"I daresay that she'll be an old quiz!" exclaimed one voice, as the door opened; a profound silence succeeded the half-finished sentence, and nothing was heard but a suppressed titter from two of the pupils as the governess entered the room.

The girls were of various ages and sizes. There was the tall Lavinia, in her own eyes a young lady quite prepared to enter the world; and, as far as acquaintance with fashionable nonsense and a taste for fine dressing could make her so, she was certainly not far wrong in her idea. She was deeper read in folly at sixteen than many a woman who has passed a long course of years in the midst of society. Her passion was love of admiration; she built her claim to it on no qualities of heart or mind that could render her an object of esteem, but on long drooping ringlets, an affected manner, and a waist squeezed into a resemblance to that of a wasp!

There was more intellect in the countenance of the pupils receiving their new governess. Carry, but it was not of the calm and noble kind produced by study and reflection. She looked rather sharp than clever; both the glance of the eye and the turn of the lip betrayed a disposition to satire, that cheapest and worst kind of wit, which makes us laugh at the expense of others. She was one who amused many, but was loved by few — had many companions, but scarcely a friend.

The pupils receiving their new governess.

Barbara was a bold, merry romp, foremost in mischief and foremost in fun, who often, from mere thoughtlessness, inflicted wounds which she neither cared nor knew how to heal. She hated books of all sorts, lessons of all kinds, and regarded a governess in the light of a jailer.

Jacqueline stood apart, a sickly, deformed girl, who mixed little in the society of her sisters; whose feeble health might have excited compassion, had not her peevish temper raised dislike.

Amy, the youngest, was a fat, good humored little child, remarkably slow in comprehension Carry used to say of her that she understood nothing, learned nothing, and remembered nothing; and that the business of a governess with her was to try and knock sparks out of a woolsack!

Such were the pupils who now received their new teacher; — Lavinia with an affected smile, and an inclination of her head on one side, till her long ringlets rested upon her neck; Carry with a criticizing glance; Barbara, a broad, bold stare. Jacqueline shrank back, looking shy and uneasy; Amy alone, when the governess courteously said, "I trust that we shall all be very good friends, when we know each other a little better," put out her fat chubby hand, and gave a broad smile in reply.

Oh, would their manners have been so cold and repulsive had they known how ached the head, how ached the heart, of her who had come among them to aid them in acquiring those treasures of know ledge which are more precious than wealth! As no one appeared disposed to speak, Mrs. Roby made another attempt to break the uncomfortable formality of the party.

"We must not think of commencing our studies till tomorrow," said she, "but I should be glad to see some of your school-books, to know what course you have been pursuing." As she spoke, she approached the table, littered over with a variety of things; and laying her hand upon the book that was nearest, read the title of a very worthless French novel.

Carry tittered; Barbara's smothered mirth forced its way in short explosive bursts, while Lavinia drew herself up with an affected air of womanly dignity, as though offended that a governess should presume to examine the character of the books which she perused.

"I must let this pass quietly this evening," thought Mrs. Roby, detaining, however, the dangerous volume, "This is not the time to find fault. I must watch the dispositions of my pupils, and know my ground, before I commence my struggle."

Unfit, indeed, did the poor lady feel for that painful, wearisome struggle. Oh! how, on that first evening passed beneath the roof of a stranger, she missed Aleck's filial attention; Bertha's tender, thoughtful care; the loving caresses of her Laura; and, most of all, the gentle, affectionate counsels of him who had been her earthly guide and support. There was no one to notice her wearied looks, no one to cheer her exhausted spirits; the sound of noisy mirth was grating to her ear; the prospect of lengthened toil, amidst those unloving, uncongenial companions, was terrible indeed to her soul She felt too ill to exert herself to be animated, too sad to rouse herself to be amusing. Glad indeed was the widow for the hour of rest.

"Do you know," whispered Carry, as, candle in hand, she accompanied Lavinia to their apartment — "do you know what is the difference between our old governess and our new one?"

"Well, our last was a much livelier individual, and dressed much more fashionably," replied the young lady.

"Yes; she appeared in flowers, and this one in weeds. I hope," she added, laughing, "that under the weeds we may not find nettles!"

Mrs. Roby retired to her own small room, and sank on her knees, exhausted. She pressed her clasped hands against her burning brow, and poured out her soul in prayer. She prayed for strength for the work before her — she prayed for success in that work. She was as the settler in a distant and desolate land, who stands in the midst of a dense forest which his hands must clear — on a dry, hard soil, which his labor must cultivate — who dares scarcely, even in hope, look forward to the day when the golden com should wave over the waste, and the blessings of home be an exile's once more!

What supported her, then, under her sense of loneliness, her consciousness of almost overwhelming difficulties be fore her? A single verse from the Scriptures, which she searched: Therefore, my beloved brethren, be ye steadfast, unmovable, always abounding in the work of the Lord, forasmuch as ye know that your labor is not in vain in the Lord. "It will not be in vain!" was the answer of faith to the promise of love: "all things are possible with God. He can make the desert blossom as the rose!"

Charlotte Maria Tucker

7. Various Paths, but One Goal

The angry thundercloud
Pours its showers on the vine,
Still in their downy shroud
Unhurt its clusters shine;
The raindrops trickle down the spray
They cannot harm, they cannot stay

On ocean the sea-mew
Fearless braves the stormy weather.
Safe in the oily dew
On each white and stainless feather
Though o'er her dash the drops of spray.
They cannot harm, they cannot stay

In hours of grief acute
Thus peace religion brings,
Like the down upon the fruit,
Or the oil upon the wings;
Though tears fall fast in sorrow's day,
They cannot harm, they cannot stay!

It was with a more serene, and even cheerful, manner that the governess met her pupils in the morning. She had, at the very out set, to speak gentle reproof; for Barbara came down with her dress in such disorder, that it was necessary to send her back to her own room; and Lavinia had risen so late, that breakfast was half finished before she appeared. This was not to be permitted, and Mrs. Roby laid down rules for the future regulation of the schoolroom, enforced by both fines and rewards; but with a disagreeable persuasion that she should have great difficulty in carrying out their execution, of which the angry looks which she now encountered were the discouraging earnest.

After breakfast the lady gathered her pupils around her, and, in a very gentle but earnest manner, told them that it had ever been her custom to commence study by the study of the volume of inspired wisdom, and a short prayer for the blessing of Heaven. The girls glanced at each other and were silent; Carry almost imperceptibly shrugging her shoulders, and Lavinia affecting to stifle a yawn. No opposition, however, was made, and the deeply impressive manner in which the widow lady read the parable of the talents, and made on it a few remarks, to stamp the lesson on the hearts of her hearers, riveted the attention even of those to whom religion had hitherto been little but a name. I know not whether any joined in the fervent prayer which succeeded; but there was One to whom it rose — by whom it was heard and accepted.

Mrs. Roby soon found that her fears were just, that she was indeed separated from her family. Her arduous duties as governess scarcely left her an hour to herself; and Lady Bunnington, a mere woman of the world, never seemed to take into consideration the yearnings of a widowed mother's heart. Mrs. Roby saw Aleck again but once, and that for a very brief space, before she found herself obliged to accompany her pupils to a fashionable watering-place, where they were to remain till the winter. "There we must leave her for a while, laboring with perseverance and patience, showing in herself a bright example of every virtue that she taught. She had not learned in vain to warn the unruly, comfort the feeble-minded, support the weak, be patient toward all men; to be not weary in well doing, but fervent in spirit, serving the Lord.

But when the widow stood with her pupils by the sea-shore, how her heart sickened as she gazed on the wide waste of heaving waters before her, and marked distant vessels tossing on the whitening surge, and heard tales of shipwreck and disaster! And how she shuddered when at night the wind howled and shrieked, as if uttering a wild wail for those who slept far away beneath the ocean! Again the blessed Scripture was her light and her hope, and she would fall asleep repeating the words, They cry unto the Lord in their trouble, and he rescues them out of their distresses; he maketh the storm a calm, so that the waves thereof are still.

Aleck was now indeed floating on the watery waste, encountering the hardships and dangers for which his former peaceful life had but ill prepared him. The quiet, studious boy was now jostled in the rough thoroughfare of the world, forced to obey promptly, act decidedly, and expose himself fearlessly and freely. It was not the meditative mind, the clear perception, which he found to be now required, but the quick eye, the ready hand, the gallant heart. And Aleck bore himself well in his new position, though suffering more from the total change in his whole mode of life, than he would have owned to any being in the world.

Two things he had resolved on before going on board, strengthening and sanctifying the resolution by prayer: —never to be ashamed of doing what was right; and never to pollute his lips with such language as he would have blushed that his dead father should hear. Against the fear of man, that brings a snare, the boy firmly and manfully wrestled; and neither the dread of ridicule nor the force of example ever led him to utter an oath. Thou God sees me! was his defense in temptation — it was also his comfort in trial; and when he stood at midnight on the sea-washed deck, and saw the pale moon gazing down from her cloudy throne, and with her soft light silvering the rolling billows, he felt it like a beautiful emblem of that religion which has power to brighten even the cloud, and cast the radiance of hope over the troubled waters of affliction!

And now we will return to poor Bertha, who, in her secluded home, has her own fight to maintain, her own cross to bear. There was something in Bertha's disposition which made carefulness and economy natural to her. This, which in the poor is a virtue, if carried to excess becomes a blemish. Mrs. Roby had warned her little daughter against selfishness; she had encouraged openness of heart and hand; she had put Bertha on her guard against an inclination to hoard up little articles that she valued a dislike to lending, and a slowness in giving, which is unworthy of the Christian character, and lowers it in the eyes of the world. But not all her mother's teaching, though poor Bertha treasured up her words in her memory, so stirred up the child's spirit against sordid meanness, so made her shrink from the idea of ever indulging it, as seeing it exemplified in Mrs. Chipstone. She was as a beacon to warn her niece from a quicksand to which circumstances might have unconsciously led her. Bertha had seen in her parents the beauty of self-denying economy; she now beheld, now suffered from, the grasping meanness of a narrow, niggardly spirit.

Mrs. Chipstone was not what would be called an irreligious woman — she was regular in prayer, and strict in the performance of many duties; but the love of gold, the' root of all evil, had so overspread her heart, that there seemed no room left in it for anything truly generous or noble. Her soul was like the prison which we read of, strangely contrived to grow narrower and narrower day by day, till it crushed its unhappy inmate between its walls. From childhood, gaining money, saving and hoarding it, had been the one ruling passion of Mrs. Chipstone. It is not one to which children are usually addicted; I speak rather, therefore, I trust, to the few than to the many, when I lift up an earnest voice against it. Oh, beware of the first symptoms of a growing love of money! a desire to possess it, to keep it, a disinclination to part with it freely! He who is close in youth is almost certain to be niggardly in age; the child who makes money his delight, may, as an old man, make it his god!

Mrs. Chipstone formed many excuses for herself; what sin is there for which the heart, which is deceitful above all things, will not discover some excuse? If she was saving, it was for her only son, the one being on earth whom she loved; she was laying up treasure for him. That he might one day be rich, there was no meanness to which she would not stoop. In order to insure his future wealth, she neglected the poor boy's present comfort. Sam had not been sent to school till even his mother felt shamed by his ignorance; and then it was for cheapness, as the first of recommendations, that she chose the seminary where she placed him. True, he had hard fare, hard treatment, hardships of all kinds to bear; but what was that, as long as Mrs. Chipstone every year placed a good round sum in the bank! "He will be glad of it one day," she would say; "we must always look forward to the future."

Mrs. Chipstone had but lately come to Grimlee, to take charge of her father-in-law's house As her Sam was the sole surviving child of his only son, she chose to consider the boy as the old gentleman's heir. This was a most unfortunate circumstance for the aged and feeble man, as Mrs. Chipstone became almost as hoarding of his money as she was of her own. She grudged firing in winter, and a doctor in sickness; clothes were expected never to wear out; the food was poor in quality, insufficient in quantity; one over-worked servant performed the labor of two.

It is true that Mrs., Chipstone herself shared the discomforts which she inflicted upon every one near her; but to her the habit of saving had become second nature, and cost her but little effort. She eared not that even a new dress always looked mean and scanty upon her, as she never bought sufficient materials for it; she cared not that her own cup at breakfast was scarcely tinged by the contents of the tea-pot, that she herself shivered beneath a threadbare shawl; — as long as she knew that she was adding to her hoarded heap she was satisfied, and approached as near towards being happy as a mind so degraded could be.

Bertha was not long in discovering by painful experience the infirmity of her aunt. One of her first annoyances was that of being obliged to replace the umbrella which she had lost, and that by a handsome silk one. "It is a useful thing to have," said Mrs. Chipstone. Bertha was at first at a loss to know why her aunt should trouble herself about the matter; but she soon found that whenever the lady took a walk, on a day when the weather was uncertain, the umbrella was gone from its peg. It was not only "useful to have," but useful to borrow; and Mrs. Chipstone appeared to regard it quite as much her own as the large faded parasol in the hall, through whose thin, tattered cover the black whalebone peered and the rain pattered in.

If Mrs. Chipstone had a letter to write, paper, envelope, even postage stamp, were borrowed from Bertha's little store. Bertha's scissors and reels of thread constantly found their way to the work-box of her aunt. But what the young girl felt most annoying was, that Mrs. Chipstone, pm-suing her economical plans, was determined to make the most of her young guest by fully employing her time.

It was a great trial to be kept from morning till night stitching a new set of curtains, till her finger became all roughened and sore. Bertha had never liked working, even for those whom she loved, and constant sitting at her needle became a real penance to the child.

She heard the birds singing without, she saw the sweet sunshine streaming in, and longed to throw aside her wearisome task and enjoy the pure breath of summer. It was with great difficulty and real self-denial that the poor girl endeavored to obey the wishes of her mother, by devoting two hours daily to study. She had to struggle against natural sloth, rise early, give up every little amusement, to find time for getting her lessons and mending the clothes which were to last her so long.

Her money, too, seemed melting away. She had to meet little expenses of which she had never dreamed; replace broken articles which she had never injured. But for the kind liberality of Mr. Gruffly she must have applied to her mother for more money, reluctant as she was to write a single word which could trouble or embarrass her parent. There was a constant pressure upon the spirits of poor Bertha, a perpetual trial to her temper. She felt tempted to dislike and despise her aunt, to call her in her heart a tyrant and a niggard; and but for the remembrance of that one constant Friend, who knew her trials and felt for her sorrows, the courage and firmness of the poor little girl would soon have entirely given way.

One evening she was sitting by the window, to avail herself of the waning light while employed over her wearisome seam, while her poor old grandfather dozed in his easy-chair beside her. To beguile the weary hours, Bertha began warbling to herself in a low tone a hymn that she loved, for it had been written by her mother, and her heavy heart needed the consolation which it contained.

Charlotte Maria Tucker

HYMN

How swiftly flies life's rapid thread,
Within the mighty loom of Time!
What brilliant tints o'er some are shed,
While some are stained with woe and crime,
But bright webs they are weaving,
Who, trusting and believing.
In scenes of sorrow, scenes of joy.
God's grace are still receiving ,

Tis thus the Christian we behold
In sickness and in woe resigned,
Because religion's thread of gold
Is in his gloomy lot entwined.
A bright web he is weaving,
When, trusting and believing.
He from a heavenly Fathers Hand
Each trial is receiving!

Death soon will snap the thread in twain
Time's busy loom itself must rest;
Nought but a winding-sheet remain
Of all that mortals e'er possest!
Then every sorrow leaving,
No more o'er trials grieving,
How blest the Christian, from his Lord
Eternal life receiving!

"That is very sweet — very sweet indeed," said a feeble voice near Bertha. "Let me hear you again, my child; I love to listen to your singing."

"Oh, grandpapa!" cried Bertha, rising and putting down the curtain, for it was now too dark to work, "I will sing to you as long as ever you like; it will be quite a pleasure to me." She seated herself at his feet, and looked up fondly into that aged face, so full of benevolence and mildness.

"I fear, my darling," said Mr. Chipstone, laying his trembling hand on her brow, "that you have but a dull time here. I have not heard you sing before."

"If I can be a comfort to you, grandpapa, it will make me happier — oh! so much happier. I can always sing at my work, and mamma has taught me a great many hymns,"

"Let's have another," said the old man, leaning back and closing his eyes; "I shall fancy that I am listening to your mother."

It was with a glow of affection and pleasure in her heart that Bertha complied, for the holy duty now set before her, of watching over and cheering the declining days of an aged Christian, was one in which an angel might have taken delight. Her voice was not powerful, but sweet; and she sang with expression, for she sang from the heart.

HYMN

The Lord, he is my strength and stay
When sorrow's cup o'erflows the brim.
It sweetens all if I can say —
It is from Him! it is from Him!

When humbly laboring for my Lord.
Faint grows the heart, and weak the limb
What strength and joy are in the word —
It is for Him! it is for Him!

I hope for ever to abide
Amid the shining seraphim.
Delivered, pardoned, glorified —
But 'tis through Him! it is through Him!

Then welcome be the hour of death,
When nature's lamp burns low and dim.
If I can cry with dying breath —
"I go to Him! I go to Him!"

She paused and glanced up at her grandfather; the old- man had sunk into a peaceful slumber!

Charlotte Maria Tucker

8. A New Acquaintance

> For in the wide world he dwells alone,
> To friendship stranger, to love unknown.

Summer had given place to autumn, the waving com assumed a golden hue, and soon the clustered sheaves dotted the field, soon the loaded wagon moved heavily along with its harvest treasure. The days grew shorter and shorter; red and yellow tints were upon the leaves, and the wind, as it blew through the woods, scattered a rustling shower. So winter came gradually on, with the morning frost and the mist of evening, till every bough became stripped and bare, and the first snow-flakes fell from the clouds. Christmas time drew near; how did it find the widow and her fatherless children?

Lady Bunnington and her family had returned to London, and Mrs. Roby had once more the joy of embracing her little Laura, seeing her look well, and bright, and happy, and as fall of affection as ever. This was a rich balm to the mother's heart; and other sources of comfort were hers. From Bertha she constantly heard, and she knew that her child was at a post which she herself would have been delighted to fill; of Bertha's trials and privations she was ignorant, therefore her heart was at rest about her. Mrs. Roby had received a letter from Aleck, dated from the Cape of Good Hope. Oh, how joyfully was that letter received! How it was read and re-read, till every sentence was known by heart!

Mrs. Roby's own quiet labors at home were not without encouragement. Her constant gentleness, her wise, judicious firmness, were making some impression even on that unpromising waste in which she had been appointed to work. True, the pleasures and follies of the world seemed to choke the good seed in Lavinia's heart — her vain mind took no interest in the things which concerned her everlasting peace: and Barbara appeared little moved; but the manners of the romp were less forward and rude, her outward appearance was altered and improved, and she looked less like an overgrown weed.

Carry was still satirical, worldly, and proud; but she was learning to think, learning that something more is required of an immortal being than quickness of repartee and sharpness of wit. She sometimes, though she never acknowledged it, felt humbled in the presence of her governess. She saw talent devoted to the glory of God; she saw calm, steady perseverance in well-doing, which was strongly contrasted with her own wayward course. Carry was not a true Christian, she had not entered on the one narrow path; but she was pausing to watch one who trod it: she admired — might she not be led to follow?

But Mrs. Roby found her greatest encouragement in the change in her two youngest pupils. Poor Jacqueline, the sickly, suffering girl, clung to her for that ready sympathy which she might not expect from her worldly mother or thoughtless sisters. Her governess was not a tyrant, but a tender, pitying friend, who guided her to the fountain of living waters, at which the weary one drank, and was refreshed. Jacqueline welcomed the message of mercy from the lips of one who had herself suffered so much. Little Amy also was readily won by Mrs. Roby's gentle and patient kindness. The hearts of the two children were given to the widow, and she received them as a precious treasure granted by God in answer to prayer.

Sweet as she felt it to be once again dwelling with those who loved her, the widow most valued her pupils' affection for the sake of the influence which it gave her over them. Her earnest desire was to win them for the Lord, to be the means of leading them to him; she longed, on the day of his appearing to meet before his throne the rejoicing spirits of those who had been her charge upon earth, and to be able to say with humble rapture, "Lo, I and the children whom thou hast given me!"

Aleck spent his Christmas in India. How strange a contrast it presented to those which he had passed at Dove's Nest! He was in Calcutta, "the city of palaces," with a thousand things around him to excite his fancy and rouse his curiosity. The dark natives of the land, the palanquins in the streets, the strange costumes, strange manners, strange climate, fruits and flowers such as he never before had beheld, all served to interest and amuse him. And yet Aleck sighed for the old joys of home; the brisk walk to church over the crackling snow, the evergreens glistening beneath their' white load, the icicles hanging from the roof, the holly-berries of scarlet and the mistletoe of white, the merry winter's evening when the ruddy fire-light shone on dear happy faces now far, far away! Aleck sat down alone in the land of strangers, and thought of his native land and friends, till his eye grew dim with tears. "They will all be thinking of me now! My mother will be praying for her sailor boy!"

But Aleck was to make no long stay in India , scarcely had the New Year commenced before he was again busy on board, amid all the bustle and excitement attending the commencement of a long voyage. But it was now with a sensation of delight that he saw the cargo stowed in the hold, luggage encumbering the deck, the passengers crowding up the sides, or bending over the bulwarks to speak last words to friends below. The cry of the sailors at the windlass, the hum of eager voices, nay, the very bleating of the sheep and cackling of the fowls which were to supply the cuddy table, all were musical in the ears of the young midshipman, for they spoke of a return to old England. There are few sensations of delight so intense as those which fill a loving heart when the anchor is weighed, and the sails spread, and the gun sounds the signal to quit a foreign shore for that of our dear native land!

But the moment of departure is not one for indulging quiet thought; bustle, confusion, hurry, were the order of the day. When the vessel was on the point of starting, it was joined by a passenger whom matters of business had detained upon shore till almost the last moment. He was a middle-aged man, with a sallow, sickly countenance, which told of long exposure to a climate which had never agreed with his constitution. Long warned by the doctors that his life might depend upon his return to a more bracing air, he had lingered and delayed, year after year, till his health was entirely broken, and at the last could scarcely be persuaded to quit his appointment in order to save his life.

There was no face, amongst all the passengers, so joyless as that of Mr. Brindley; home seemed for him to have no attractions — he cared not to return to his country. Perhaps he had no friends to welcome him there — perhaps during his long absence every tie had been broken, or he might have learned to consider that foreign land as his home in which he had lingered so long — like one who, fixing his heart upon things of earth, looks on the world as his rest, forgetful of a better country above, or dreading to be called to depart for that land where he dares not hope to find a welcome!

Mr. Brindley stumbled as he stepped upon deck, either from his weakness or his haste. Aleck assisted him to rise, and showed to the invalid such little attentions as his helpless state required. This was the commencement of a sort of acquaintance between the passenger and the boy. Not that Aleck felt drawn towards Mr. Brindley by any feeling but that of compassion. Neither what he saw of him, nor what he heard of him from others, inclined Aleck either to like or respect him. He was prodigiously rich, it was said — had shaken the pagoda tree to some purpose; by which was meant, that he had contrived, by some means or other, to make a good deal of money from the natives. With his stooping gait, shuffling step, and eye which always avoided meeting that of another, his gloomy look, his almost timid manner, he gave the young midshipman the idea of one who bore with him a burdened conscience. Riches, it was clear, did not make him happy — what if they should be at the root of his sadness!

Aleck was confirmed in this suspicion by a slight incident which occurred some days after the vessel had sailed from Calcutta.

He was talking to a young messmate upon deck one evening, not observing that Mr. Brindley was near, coiled up in shawls and wrappers, inhaling the cool sea-breeze, which brought no freshness or color to his faded cheek.

"I say, Roby, I suppose that you don't go home empty-handed," said Jack Churton, Aleck's messmate and companion, "I'm taking home a pretty sight of curiosities, as well as a green parrot. Have you something stowed away in your locker?"

"Well," replied Aleck, "I have bought some trifles, specimens of the workmanship of the country. I was tempted to spend my last shilling upon them."

And, in fact, one of the greatest pleasures of the boy had been that of collecting little remembrances for his mother and sisters, and imagining the delight with which Bertha and Laura would examine his treasures from India.

"You'll have to pay duty for them," carelessly observed Jack.

Aleck was startled: he had never thought of that. "If they will not let them pass at the custom-house, they must just keep them," said he, in a tone of disappointment, "for all my money is gone already."

"Tut, Tut, we'll get them through," said Jack, good-naturedly. "I suppose the articles aren't very bulky — don't require much stowage-room?"

"No; they are merely little scarfs, and such things."

"Well, wind them round your waist, my good fellow; they'll not be seen through your blue jacket; and you just look innocent, and go boldly past the officers. I warrant you they'll never suspect you."

"What! — smuggle!" exclaimed Aleck, indignantly.

"There's no harm in it; every one does it. The government doesn't want your shillings. Who'll be the worse, I should like to know?"

"I should be the worse," said Aleck, quietly.

"I don't think all the treasures of India worth one falsehood or one fraud."

"Trash and nonsense!" muttered Jack, sauntering angrily away,

"You are right! You are right!" exclaimed a voice near, and to Aleck's surprise Mr. Brindley laid a trembling hand on his arm. "Keep those principles, boy; they are those which I was taught when a child. Hold them fast," he added, in a more agitated tone, "then will you never know the curse which clings to ill-gotten gold, and eats into the soul like a canker."

The invalid sank back again on his seat, and turned away his head, as if ashamed of having been betrayed into uttering words which might bear a construction unfavorable to himself. But these earnest impassioned words had raised in Aleck's breast a feeling of melancholy interest in the stranger, and he remembered him that night in his prayers.

Notwithstanding the feebleness of his health, Mr. Brindley was never absent when the ship's crew assembled for divine service. But it was noticed by those whose slight attention to the sermon left them leisure to remark the demeanor of others, that his pale cheek grew paler, and that there was an uneasy twitch in his upper lip, which betrayed some secret emotion, when the clergyman who preached gave out his first solemn text, What shall it profit a man if he gain the whole world and lose his own soul? Or what shall a man give in God in exchange for his soul?

Charlotte Maria Tucker

MR. BRINDLEY AND ALECK.

9. Winter at Grimlee

Pray with thanksgiving; as the lark in air
Pours music as he soars beyond our gaze,

Not only mount upon the wing of prayer,
But breathing notes of gratitude and praise.

Winter brought with it peculiar trials to Bertha. The shortened daylight was to her shortened time; for Mrs. Chipstone grudgingly gave the smallest allowance of candle, and the child would repeat to herself, before rising, French verbs, dates, and tables, when it was too dark for her to read, and before a fire was lighted in the house. If she sometimes dropped asleep over the task, I hope that ray reader will account it no great crime.

But Bertha was gradually becoming more reconciled to her position at Grimlee. She doubted whether, even if it were in her power to do so, she should quit the home of her poor old grandfather. She would sit for hours, when her aunt had no work for her to do, gently chafing his feet till she brought warmth to them. She placed his pillow as no One else could place it, prepared his gruel, read to him, sang to him, and made it her delight to minister to the infirmities of age. And filial piety brings its own peculiar reward. The blessing of Heaven rests on the dutiful child. Happy are those who, led by the Spirit of God, keep the first commandment with a promise.

Bertha looked forward with pleasure to the time of Christmas, as her cousin would come home for the holidays, and she longed for a companion of her own age. She had never seen Samuel, but his mother spoke fondly of him — even her cold dry manner thawed when her boy was the subject of conversation.

"Even if I should not like him much," thought Bertha, "I will remember how I felt towards the Probyns — what torments they were to me at first, and how they gradually improved, till at last I was really sorry to lose them. And oh, if Sam should be like my Aleck! —that is almost too much to hope for. But whatever he is, his coming will be a break on the dullness and silence of this house, and who knows whether aunt may not make things more comfortable when her only son is at home!"

There was some truth in this last conjecture On the day of Sam's expected arrival, the new curtains replaced the old ones, which were almost falling to pieces; Mrs. Chipstone put on coals with the shovel instead of the tongs, and stirred the fire into something like a blaze, and prepared such dainties for the table as Bertha had not seen since her arrival at Grimlee. The day was bright and cheerful Mrs. Chipstone put on her old shawl and clogs, and started herself for the station to welcome her son.

Bertha sat by the window and watched; her spirits felt lighter than they had done since the death of her father. A letter from Mrs. Roby, that morning received, enclosing a copy of Aleck's, had filled her heart with joy. Her grandfather had spoken to her some of those sweet words which are treasured up in memory, and remain a source of pure, holy pleasure, long after the lips which uttered them are silent and cold. "How pleasant it is," said a holy man, "when the bird in the bosom sings sweetly!"

Bertha was not kept very long waiting, though impatience made time appear to go slowly. Her aunt returned with her son, a tall, high-shouldered boy, with red hair, weak eyes, and a dull, cheerless expression of face.

"This horrid snow!" were the first words which he uttered on entering the house, as he stamped upon the mat to shake it off" his boots.

"How I do detest winter! And there were never such roads as we have here."

Mrs. Chipstone introduced him to his cousin. Sam shook hands with Bertha awkwardly, but kindly, swinging his arm like the handle of a pump.

"How glad you must feel to be at home again," said Bertha.

"Oh, anything's better than that odious school! But I don't like the country at all — it's so dreary, and so miserably cold."

Bertha soon discovered that the cheerfulness of her life at Grimlee would be little increased by the society of poor Sam. She remembered that her father used playfully to say of his wife, that she saw everything through rose-colored spectacles — the brightness of her own spirit cast such light on all around, she was so ready to hope and to admire. But Sam's spectacles must have been of the most somber and gloomy hue, for everything appeared wrong in his eyes. It was not that he was an ill-disposed boy: he was not untruthful, ungenerous, nor unkind. There was little cause of complaint against him but this, that he himself was always complaining. He seemed to carry bad weather with him, and discomfort followed him like a shadow.

Sam made Bertha quite dismal with his dreadful accounts of what he had to endure at school — how he was flogged by the master, worried by the usher, hunted by the boys, over-worked, under-fed, and neglected. Bertha wondered that Mrs. Chipstone did not remove him from such a school; and so she probably would have done, could she have found another equally cheap. But had Sam been in a palace, he would have been miserable still; a repining, unthankful temper would have embittered the sweetest cup. Those who "seek for thorns" will assuredly "find their share;" and no pleasure on earth can render those happy who are determined to find a fault in everything.

On Christmas, Sam showed Bertha a pencil-case, which he had received that morning from his mother.

"What a beauty!" exclaimed his cousin in admiration, secretly wondering at the unwonted liberality of her aunt.

"It's well enough," said Sam, twisting it round and round with a discontented air; "but I wish that mother had spoken to me before she bought it I should much rather have had a good knife. Besides, I hate these patent concerns; one is always losing the leads. It will be of no use to me at all"

"But look at the beautiful seal at the end of the pencil-case," said Bertha,

"It's only the impression of a flower, heart's-ease, too, such an ugly, common thing; as if I would ever seal a letter with that."

"Heart's-ease is a very good thing," said Bertha, playfully; "and it is not common either, I'm afraid. But now that you've shown me your present, I will show you mine. You will see that my own dear mother and sister have not forgotten me," And, with a face radiant with smiles. Bertha drew forth the little treasures which she had that day received. "Look at these nice cuffs: they are all mammas' own work; and grandpapa has a pair something like them. They will keep us so comfortable and warm,"

"They are of a very ugly color," remarked Sam,

"Do you think so?" said Bertha, a little disappointed; "but it is an excellent color for wearing."

"And what is the use of this two-penny-halfpenny concern?" asked Sam, taking up a neat little marker.

"That is dear Laurie's present to me. Little darling! I will always use it for her sake."

"I don't see the use of markers; where is the advantage of reading if one cannot even remember one's place in the book? Did you ever hear the story of the Irishman who was reading a volume and some good-natured person put back his marker every day to the place from which he started, so that he was always reading the same thing over and over?"

"And did he not find out the joke?"

"No; the stupid fellow, he did not. When asked his opinion of the book, he said that he thought it excellent, only that there was a good deal of repetition in it."

Bertha was amused at the anecdote, and told Sam that she should be on her guard lest he played the same trick upon her.

Bertha sometimes really pitied her aunt, when she saw the vain efforts made by Mrs. Chipstone to render her son happy at home. Nothing that she did ever called forth a smile, a word of thanks, or apparently a feeling of gratitude. Whether she sat straining her eyes by the one dim candle making or mending his apparel, or wearied her brain devising some little amusement to cause his holidays to pass more pleasantly, or hinted to him the daily sacrifices which she endured for his future comfort, he took all as a matter of course, without showing either thankfulness or affection. And the same disposition which made him cold and ungrateful towards an earthly parent rendered him the same towards his heavenly Father.

He never considered how much greater were his blessings than his deserts. How different was his position from that of the fatherless girl whom his mother treated as a dependent, and who yet could say, not only with her lips, but from her heart, I will bless the Lord at all times: his praise shall continually be in my mouth! He never thanked the Almighty for the blessings of creation — for sight, hearing, and speech, for health of body, for the precious difficulties of the mind. He never thanked the Lord for yet more wondrous mercies — for the means of grace, and for the hope of glory, for transgressions pardoned, for heaven purchased with the life's blood of God's only Son!

Reader, is it thus with you? Do petty cares weigh you down, petty sorrows overwhelm? Is the sunshine of life overclouded with discontent — do you receive God's blessings with a thankless spirit, and murmur under every trial which he sends you? The ancients said that the ungrateful man had but one sin, since ingratitude was one so hateful that all others beside it were forgotten. And do you think that your forgetfulness of benefits is less sinful because they are more than you can number, or your ingratitude a thing less odious because shown towards an Almighty Benefactor?

Bertha grieved over the repining temper of her cousin, and made many a fruitless attempt to rouse the boy to cheerfulness. She knew no better remedy for gloom and discontent than religion, for she had herself proved its power to brighten the darkest trials of life; and she trusted and prayed that a beam of its radiance might shine on her cousin, as on one dark cold Sunday evening she sang to him the following hymn: —

HAPPINESS.

Can happiness be found
By mortals? Wherefore not?
Though its full, living tide, we know,
Before God's throne alone can flow.
Much of its mingling stream below

Sweetens the Christian's lot.
They who their Savior's love possess,
Have they no source of happiness?
The world with envy views

The heir to vast domains.
And sighs his happiness to share.
But happier, oh! beyond compare,
The man to heaven itself the heir,
Where bliss eternal reigns!
While hope points onward to thy rest,

Oh, heir of Heaven, art thou not blest

How happy he whose youth
A tender parent guides!
But Christians have a Sire above
At once all power and all love;
Time cannot change him, death remove,—
He for each want provides.
Though by the whole world scorned, oppressed
Oh, child of God, art thou not blest?

The captive debtor's heart
Glows with delight indeed,
When from his hands the fetters fall,
His debts forgiven, cancelled all. —
Oh thou, redeemed from Satan's thrall,
Delivered, pardoned, freed,
Glows there no rapture in thy breast?
Ransomed of Christ I art thou not blest?

With rapturous delight
The exile homeward turns!
A fairer land before our eyes
In bright and vivid prospect lies;
Each moment nearer to the skies.
The home for which he yearns.
Though tossing still on ocean's breast,
Is not the heaven-bound Christian blessed

Then shame upon the tear
The world has power to wring!
Check, check the vain, ungrateful sigh.
He who for man vouchsafed to die.
Will naught, save what may harm, deny
Light shall from darkness spring!
In songs of praise exalt thy voice;
Rejoice — be thankful and rejoice!

Charlotte Maria Tucker

10. The Post

The clock, whose chime at Intervals we hear,
Resembles friendship's warning to the ear;

Its hand, to truth still pointing silently,
Example's ceaseless lesson to the eye!

What! There's the postman!" cried Constantine.

"I wonder that you're not rushing off to examine what is in the letter-box," said his brother, stretching himself on his easy-chair, and looking as though it would take no slight motive to move him to rise.

"Oh! It's not likely that it holds anything for me. I heard from Bertha yesterday."

"Any news?" inquired Adolphus with a yawn. "Her cousin returned last week to school in very low spirits, she says."

"Poor fellow, I'm sorry for him. It's a good thing for us that papa has given us another half-year at home."

"A pleasant thing, I daresay. I am not quite so sure if it really is a good thing. You want a bit of the spur to make you get on with your studies,"

"And you want a bit of the rein to bridle that tongue of yours," laughed Adolphus. "But let's hear the letter of Bertha."

"Well," said Constantine, drawing it from his pocket, "that postman's knock brought it to my mind As Bertha had not much news to put into her note, she filled it up by copying out some verses of her mother's. I fancy," he added, smiling, "that Bertha is afraid that I may forget here some of the lessons which I learned at Dove's Nest; but her own conduct towards me was a lesson which I believe that I shall remember as long as I live."

"But what has that to do with the postman?"

"The poetry is called 'The Postman's Song;' and as often as I hear the double knock, I daresay that I shall think of the verses."

"An odd subject for poetry, I should call it," said Adolphus, as he unfolded the letter which Constantine handed to him, and read.

THE POSTMAN'S SONG

Day after day my constant course I keep,
Much wished-for oft, yet never asked to stay;
Nor know I who may laugh, or who may weep.
While gazing on the tidings I convey.
So there is one who comes to rich and poor;
Expected long, unwelcome though he be.
When Death's loud knock is sounding at my door,
My God! What tidings will he bring to me?

The worldly man to vast possessions heir;
The selfish man, whose treasure is below,
The covetous, absorbed in earthly care; —
To such his tidings are of grief and woe.
Thieves, Sabbath-breakers, scoffing at God's Word,
Who rush on paths which conscience must condemn
When Death's loud knock is at their dwellings heard.
Oh! fearful tidings must he bring to them!

The pardoned penitent, redeemed from sin;
The lowly one, whose treasure is above;
The pure, who seek a heavenly crown to win; —
To such his tidings are of peace and love.
He comes to tell them that their griefs are o'er,
That Christ from sin and sorrow sets them free!
When Death's loud knock is sounding at my door,
Such blissful tidings may he bring to me!

Adolphus looked grave as he returned the letter but he made no observation upon it.

The servant entered with a letter upon a salver.

"Well, there is one for me! — Who would have thought it?" cried Constantine; "and I'm sure that the writing is Mrs. Roby's. What can she be writing about to me, I wonder!" He hastily broke the seal, and exclaimed, "Why, if she has not sent me four halves of five-pound notes!"

"The other halves will follow when she hears that these have been received," said Adolphus. "I suppose that she is returning the money which you sent her."

"All! She wrote last summer that she only accepted it as a loan it's so like her. I only hope that she has not been denying herself comforts in order to save up the sum. I never dreamed of her sending it so soon,"

"Do you consider the money yours?" said Adolphus, dryly.

"Well, why, I don't exactly know. I believe that it will be the most honorable thing to carry the bank-notes to my father."

"You may depend upon it he will give you the watch now," said Adolphus, with a little vexation in his manner. "I might just as well have waited for mine, for I broke the mainspring yesterday."

With a feeling of elation Constantine hastened to the study of his father, and, without saying a word, put Mrs. Roby's envelope and its enclosures into his hand.

"This is a very handsome note," said the gentleman, after perusing a letter which accompanied the money. "Mrs. Roby shows very lady-like feeling — very. It's a pleasure to have aided so estimable ft person in her time of necessity." Mr. Probyn pulled up his shirt collar as he spoke, with an uncommonly self-satisfied air. "And now," he added, smiling, "what do you expect me to do with these twenty pounds?"

"Well — papa," Constantine hesitated, and then laughed.

"I must get you a watch with the half of it; but here is enough of money for two. You have got good interest for your gold! But you'll not want two watches, I should say. Shall we get a gold chain, seal, and key?"

"Oh! Papa, if you are really so kind as to give me a choice, I would rather, much rather have two watches!"

"Hey! One on either side, to keep the balance true?" laughed Mr. Probyn.

"No; one for myself, and one for Bertha. You know that I really owe her a debt of gratitude; she was so good to me when I was almost blinded; so patient, so forgiving, so self-denying! I should like to show her that I remember kindness; and more especially now that she is so poor."

"Well, my boy, the money is yours; I never take back a present. You may order the two watches when you please."

With a light step, and lighter heart, Constantine quitted the study. "I do believe," thought he, "that it is quite true that we never shall repent doing a kind act, Adolphus never will look upon his watch with half the pleasure with which I shall look upon mine! And Bertha — how much surprised and delighted she will be! And then to receive such a letter from Mrs. Roby, and know that I really did help her through her difficulties — I'm not sure if that is not the best part of it all!"

The Battle (Illustrated)

11. The Past Brightens the Present

In fonder yaw, replenished by the shower,
Pour the rich wine; it spreads as it descends,

Parades the whole, and with mysterious power
To every drop Its hue and sweetness lends:

Thus should Religion's influence serene
Be felt in every thought, in every action seen.

February, the last winter month, had commenced with more than its usual severity. The milk congealed in the pail, the water in the pitcher, the pump was loaded with clustering icicles. The days were lengthening, indeed, but the dull, red sun appeared to shed no warmth over the icy world. Poor Bertha was almost frozen in her cheerless home at Grimlee. Her grandfather, suffering from severe cold, was now confined to his room; and Bertha felt bitterly, that though he had everything that was actually necessary for his comfort, there were many little indulgences which his age and infirmities required, and which affection would have anxiously supplied, which were denied him by the cold parsimony of his daughter-in-law.

Bertha was also hurt by the manner of Mrs. Chipstone towards the invalid. She treated him almost as a child, never consulted his wishes, and seemed to regard him as one whose failing intellect made his opinion a matter of no importance. Bertha sometimes fancied that the feeble old man was almost afraid of her aunt; and that she, on her part, regarded him rather as an encumbrance, a troublesome charge, than as a venerable parent, to whose declining years it should be her privilege and pleasure to minister. And oh, how Bertha pined to be once more, if but for one hour, with her mother! She felt as though that mother's smile would bring summer again into her heart. When, when would they meet again? For how long was this dreary winter of trial to last?

With such thoughts as these chilling her young heart, and filling her eyes with tears, Bertha sat in the little parlor, beside the fireless grate; for it was a rule of Mrs. Chipstone's that the fire should never be lighted till the last thing before breakfast. Bertha was glad to see Nancy enter with the wood and candle, and make preparations for raising a scanty glow amongst the embers which remained from the fire of yesterday, carefully raked together. The poor servant-girl's fingers trembled with cold; she had a hungry and half-frightened look, as one who was more familiar with sharp words than with hearty meals. She would have been a great trial, it must be owned, to patience more exemplary than that of Mrs. Chipstone, being one of the dullest and most ignorant girls in the county, slow to learn and quick to forget, and only kept in her place because she was one who would work hard and expect little wages.

Now, amongst the many orders given to Nancy, but always forgotten by her, was one never to place a lighted candle on the floor. She forgot it now, as she knelt down to arrange the wood in the grate, and Bertha was just about to remind her of the charge, when Mrs. Chipstone's voice was heard from the top of the stairs, impatiently calling for the maid. Nancy started up as she heard her name called, and forgetting, in her haste to obey the summons, where she had placed the candle, she moved so close to it that a draught of air through the open door blew her cotton dress right against the light, and in a moment the poor girl was in flames!

Ignorant, terrified out of even the very small share of sense which she possessed, Nancy could do nothing but run about and scream; and it was well for her that some one was near who retained presence of mind. Bertha had heard from her mother what was the proper course to pursue in such a case; she snatched up the rug from the hearth, hastily pressed it over the burning dress, and in less time than I have taken to relate the occurrence, the flames were extinguished, and the poor servant stood frightened, trembling, but perfectly uninjured!

Mrs. Chipstone, finding her call unanswered, entered the room at that minute, A glance showed her what had happened; but instead of sharing the thankful joy of Bertha Roby at the preservation of a fellow-creature from so horrible a fate, she first angrily chid Nancy for her carelessness and disobedience, and then fixed her eyes upon the rug, which had been singed in putting out the fire.

"You know the rule of the house," she said coldly to her niece; "those who spoil things are expected to replace them."

"But, aunt," expostulated poor Bertha.

"No words; I have said it; that is enough,"

But this cruel load upon the orphan's scanty resources was too glaringly unjust not to be resisted a little longer. "What could I have done, aunt?" cried Bertha, the blood mounting to her cheek; "you would not punish me for trying to save poor Nancy; that would be very — " she stopped herself, barely in time, for a word trembled on her lips, which, if uttered, would have brought on her the stern anger of one who had but too much power to make that anger felt. As it was, Mrs. Chipstone merely said, as she turned coldly away, "You have destroyed the rug, and you must pay for it."

The breakfast was a very silent one. Bertha's heart was swelling with such anger and indignation that she felt as though her food would choke her. When the meal was ended, and Mrs. Chipstone had quitted the room to carry some tea to the invalid, Bertha again seated herself close by the fireplace, and buried her face in her hands. She felt much inclined to weep passionately, but she struggled against her emotion. She had never been so violently angry since Constantine had fought and knocked down her brother Aleck, in the days of his untamed wildness.

"Mean, unjust, heartless, wicked! Oh, how I hate and despise her!" Such were the evil thoughts which rushed like a flame through the heart of the child, and, but for the power of religion, would have spread, furious and unchecked sweeping away every vestige of inward peace.

But Bertha knew that her passion was sinful, and she had learned where to turn for its cure. Pray for them that despitefully use you. Forgive, and ye shall be forgiven. Could she forget whose lips had uttered these words? Who had given the command, and would help his weak child to fulfill it? Bertha sank on her knees, and clasped her hands. "Oh, forgive me, and forgive her!" was all that she could say; but she repeated her brief prayer over and over, till she became more calm; the fierce fire within was gradually extinguished, and before she arose from her knees, her prayer was changed into humble thanksgiving for having been made the means of saving the poor servant.

"That is a pleasure not to be bought with money," she thought, as, again seated, she prepared to commence her daily task of needle-work. "I would not part with it for all the gold that my aunt has, or ever will have. It was very wrong in me to be so angry with her. I thought, at Dove's Nest, that I was learning to subdue my passionate feelings; but I suppose that, all through my life, I shall be discovering more and more how weak and sinful I am. It is a long, long battle; but then to think of the victory, and the crown!"

Bertha's reflections were interrupted by the entrance of Nancy. "Here's a man from the station. Miss," said she, "who has brought a paper for Missus, and a little parcel for you; and he's waiting to be paid."

"A parcel for me!" cried Bertha, as she hastily drew money from her purse, and dismissed the girl, who, before carrying the paper to her mistress, stopped to have a long gossip with the ploughman messenger, visitors being very rare at Grimlee.

"A parcel for me!" repeated Bertha, "and directed, 'Glass, handle with great care'. "Who can have sent it? What can it contain?" Great was her astonishment when, coverings of brown paper and white being removed, and a small red morocco case opened, she beheld a treasure which she had never hoped to possess, a beautiful little gold watch!

I need hardly describe her surprise and delight at receiving a gift so unexpected. But it was a deeper pleasure than that of a child on whom a beautiful toy has been bestowed, or of an older person becoming possessor of something essential to comfort, that made the eyes of Bertha sparkle, as she read Constantine's accompanying note: —

"Dear Bertha, —

I hope that you will kindly wear this little watch, in remembrance of the time when you fairly won the victory over a very troublesome enemy, by pelting him with benefits, as Fides the giant-killer did his foes! I have now a watch of my own; but to wear it gives me less pleasure than to send this to you. — Yours,

CONSTANTINE PROBYN."

"Dear little watch!" exclaimed Bertha, "how I shall value it! I have never known exactly how time went here, as my aunt's old watch is always wrong, and there is no clock but in the kitchen; but now — oh, how useful it will be! I shall learn to be punctual at last. And I hope that I shall learn something better still, — that it will remind me to be patient and long-suffering, when I remember what dear Con was once, and what he is now! Oh, we should never leave off" waiting, and hoping, and praying! When I feel angry in future, the short hand of my watch shall remind me to be slow to anger, and the long one to be quick to forgive."

The sun, bursting from a cloud, poured a bright, cheerful ray into the room, and lighted up the landscape without, sparkling on the icicles which hung from the eaves, till they glittered like diamonds. The sudden beam was quite in accordance with the pleasant emotions called up in the bosom of Bertha; and as she placed her watch beside her, and resumed her work, the hymn with which she beguiled the time was one which the sunshine within and without naturally suggested to her memory.

HYMN.

The great I envy not,
Nor seek what worldlings prize;
Mine is a brighter lot,
Whose home is in the skies!
To pride it may be sweet,
Rank, riches to possess: —
To lie at Jesus' feet,

This, this is happiness!
What are the cares of life?
Soon, soon all cares will cease;
Above the world's vain strife
The Christian soars in peace.
Trials in vain annoy.
While to the Cross we press;
Earth has its fading joy,
But this is happiness!

Oh! May I part with all,
Ere I such hopes resign;
Lord, keep me, lost I fall.
Nor let my faith decline!
To rest on thee alone,
To feel thy power to bless
To live and die thine own, —
This, this is happiness!

Mrs. Chipstone sank on a chair, and wept tears of anguish.

Bertha's closing notes were interrupted by something like a cry from the rooms above. She started up, fearing lest something should have befallen her grandfather; but ere she could reach the door, Mrs. Chipstone, pale as ashes, rushed in, with a telegraph paper in her hand.

"My boy! My boy!" she exclaimed, and sinking on a chair, wept such tears of anguish as Bertha had hardly believed that these cold, unfeeling eyes could have shed.

The paper contained a message, brief and blunt, as telegraph messages usually are: —

"S. Chipstone is dangerously ill. Come, if you wish to see him alive."

But these few words conveyed to the mother's heart a world of misery and fear. They told that the one earthly pillar on which her hopes rested was shaking, perhaps soon to fall; that the son for whom she had been saving and hoarding might be now on the brink of the grave, where gold and silver are worthless trash; that her wealth was vanity — her wisdom worse than folly!

Bertha really felt for her aunt, in that hour of deep distress, when the pure consolations which support the suffering Christian had no power to raise her from despair. All that Bertha could do for Mrs. Chipstone was to aid her in making preparations for a hasty journey, and to promise, to the utmost of her power, to take her aunt's place in watching over her grandfather.

So the miserable mother departed, carrying her little bundle through the snow herself for she would not incur the expense of hiring a porter; and Bertha, after watching her as she hurried along the road, dark and slippery with ice, returned from the window to offer up an earnest prayer for her suffering cousin and his afflicted parents

The Battle (Illustrated)

12. A Difficult Position

What once was moss see petrified to stone;
Life, texture gone, the form remains alone,
And hardens not the world, by process slow.
Hearts fixed where its enchanted waters flow?
The form of godliness may yet remain,
But can the worldly heart its power retain?

In the day following that on which the occurrences related in the last chapter took place at Grimlee, Mrs. Roby sat alone in the school-room in Grosvenor Place, making brief notes of the sermon which heard that afternoon at church. The preacher had discoursed on worldliness, had shown its terrible power gradually to harden the heart, and for every generous, every holy emotion, substitute one hateful image of self.

To the widow the subject was now one of peculiar interest; for every week was disclosing more and more the worldly character of Sir John Bunnington and his wife. Mrs., Roby knew that her pupils were living in an unwholesome atmosphere — that they could scarcely avoid imbibing evil principles from those with whom they associated. Her anxiety on their account had lately been greatly increased by the return of their brother, a young officer, from his regiment. Lively, handsome, but, alas utterly unprincipled, he could not but exert most dangerous influence over the impressible minds of his sisters.

He instilled into them his own passion for gaiety and excitement; he laughed at scruples, and only treated with ridicule every attempt to lead their minds to higher thoughts. He quizzed the governess, drew caricatures of her, encouraged the girls to dispute her authority and neglect her commands; and though he could not succeed in rooting out the good seed so carefully planted in the hearts of his younger sisters, he confused their ideas of right and wrong; while with Lavinia he utterly destroyed every vestige of religious training. He was doing the evil one's work in his home with only too great success!

Lady Bunnington had put off her grand entertainments till her son's return and the meeting of Parliament. Both these events had now taken place, and cards of invitation were sent in all directions. The lady remembered that the members of the House of Commons, engaged in their public duties, had no evenings free for social meetings but those of Saturday and Sunday. They were certain to have so many invitations for the former day, that she usually fixed on the latter for her large dinner parties, to the deep distress of Mrs. Roby, who found herself placed in a great strait, unwilling either to appear by silence to countenance a sin, or to induce her pupils, even in thought, to condemn the conduct of the parents whom they should honor.

As she sat writing, but with thoughts often wandering to the peculiar difficulties of her position, little Amy came softly into the room, and, closing the door behind her, came to the side of her governess.

"Are you busy, or may I speak to you a little?"

"I am always ready to hear you, my love," said Mrs. Roby, laying down her pen with a secret fear of what the child might be going to say.

"You know we've a great party to-day —"

"I know it," replied the governess.

"Is it right to ask so many people on Sunday?" said the child, fixing her eyes on the face of the widow.

"It is not your place, dear Amy, to discuss that question at present. You have nothing to do with the inviting; simply think what is your own duty in the world."

"But it is about my own duty that I am puzzled," said the little girl, drawing closer to Mrs. Roby, and glancing round to see that she was not overheard. "Mamma says that we are all, except Jacqueline, to come down after dinner; and then Hugh is determined that we shall all sing that funny chorus — you know which I mean — the one which you accompany on the piano; that is his favorite of all our pieces. And I told him that I should not like to sing that on Sunday, and he laughed, and joked, and teased me, and promised to make me dance a shawl dance all by myself; and now, what am I to do?"

Mrs. Roby found it very hard to meet the appealing look of that trusting little face. She bent down to kiss it before she replied: "I will speak to your mamma, dear, about it. I hope that she will not allow you to be teased for not doing what you think wrong."

"But if she does wish the chorus, will you play to our singing?"

"No!" said Mrs. Roby, rising from her seat. She sought her own room for prayer and reflection. She alike dreaded deserting her post, forsaking the poor children in so dangerous a position, or making any sacrifice of her own duty as a Christian. It seemed to her that but one right course was before her — gently, meekly, but earnestly to expostulate with Lady Bunnington herself.

The interview was likely to be a very trying one to the governess, poor, despised, dependent; but she nerved herself for it by prayer. She then glided to the apartment where Lady Bunnington was preparing her toilette for her grand entertainment.

The lady, wrapped in a rich dressing-gown, was seated at her glass; articles of jewelry and various ornaments were spread in glittering array before her. A scent of perfumes pervaded the room. The maid flitted here and there, bringing one after another splendid pieces of dress from a large mahogany wardrobe.

"Might I request a few moments of private conversation with you?" said Mrs. Roby.

"If there is anything of importance," — the lady glanced at her mirror. "Lepine, you may retire; " and the maid, with a little flippant toss of the head at the interruption from a governess, quitted the apartment.

"Anything that concerns the children?" asked Lady Bunnington, after a painful pause, during which the widow was anxiously pondering in what way to commence. There was something freezing in the tone of the lady, and yet more in the appearance of her stiff, stately form, the proud neck and haughty mien.

"Yes; indeed it deeply concerns the children," replied Mrs. Roby; and then, very gently, but in simple, forcible language she expressed the impossibility of leading her pupils in the right way without the encouragement and assistance of their parents, or to make the fifth commandment appear sacred in their eyes, if they were suffered to disregard the obligation of the fourth. She spoke of the sacredness, the blessedness of the Sabbath, its influence on the whole of week-day life; she besought the mother, with all the earnestness of a mother, to make the path of duty plain and straight before her children, to let them connect thoughts of home with thoughts of heaven, that they might all spend an eternal Sabbath together, a family "unbroken, in the skies."

Lady Bunnington listened in stately silence, uttering nothing but an occasional hard, dry cough. When Mrs. Roby had concluded her appeal, she coldly said, "You have your opinions and I have mine; I desire to hear no more upon this subject."

"But this evening —"

"This evening I expect you to assist my daughters in entertaining my guests with music." She turned towards her glass, and took up a jewel-case, as though to signify that she considered the conversation at an end.

"Madam," said Mrs. Roby, "would you expect, would you even wish, that I, the widow of a clergyman" — her Lip trembled as she spoke — "should show an example of inconsistency to the principles which he taught, before the children whom you have confided to me to train?"

"Well, really, Mrs. Roby," said Lady Bunnington, with a quicker, sharper manner than before, "I think it better that we should understand each other distinctly. It seems to me that you have somewhat mistaken your place; I am, and will always be, mistress in my own house. We part this day, month or sooner if you please."

The governess bowed in silence and withdrew. Lady Bunnington rang for her maid.

Was this, then, the answer to the widow's prayer? Was this the reward of her adherence to duty? She was again to be thrown on the world's wide sea; she was to leave her poor lambs in the very midst of temptations which she dared scarcely hope that they would have strength to resist. Would it not have been better to have yielded a little, dissembled a little — to have followed the world outwardly, and contented herself with serving God silently and in secret?

Conscience gave a solemn "No" to the question it is only want of faith which can ever lead a Christian to do evil that good may come. God needs not our sin to work his own good purposes. Notwithstanding the grief felt by some of the family when they heard that their governess was to leave them, notwithstanding the loss which they incurred in the departure of one who had devoted herself to promoting their best welfare, even to the daughters of Lady Bunnington good was brought out of seeming evil.

The sacrifice of Mrs. Roby for conscience' sake made a deeper impression on the minds of her younger pupils than years of instruction might have done. They saw the reality of the power of religion, and when the conduct and character of Mrs. Roby were spoken of, even the satirical Carry could not sneer. From the day when she wept parting tears on the bosom of her friend, Jacqueline gave herself entirely to the Lord, and she remained in her worldly home one of God's hidden ones; or rather as a little missionary, exerting quiet influence in her domestic circle; and never forgetting to pray, mom and eve, for the beloved instructress who had first led her to rejoice in her Savior!

As I shall not have further occasion to introduce Lady Bunnington or her family into ray tale, I may as well mention here, before we quit the subject, that Lavinia's making an early and very foolish marriage, without the consent or even knowledge of her parents, and Hugh's being publicly disgraced for some gambling transaction, greatly humbled the pride and broke the spirit of their mother. She took a distaste for society, buried herself and her family in the country, and perhaps secretly regretted, though she never owned that she did so, that she had driven from her daughters a safe and faithful guide, who, in teaching them to reverence their God, would have also taught them to honor their parents.

As regarded Mrs. Roby herself, though she could not at first but feel distressed at thus losing, at least for a time, the means of supporting herself and helping her children, when she on the next morning received a letter from Grimlee, and learned that her father was unwell, her sister-in-law gone, her Bertha left alone in charge of the house and the invalid, she was thankful for the freedom which enabled her to go herself where her presence was so much required. Under other circumstances she might have been uncertain what course it would be wise to pursue, but she saw the leading of Providence in those unforeseen events which had rendered her way so plain. And certainly if conscience pointed now to the sick-room at Grimlee as her post of duty, it was the spot of all others upon earth to which inclination would have led her; and the widow felt happier than she had ever thought that her bereaved heart could have been again in this world, when she was locked in her venerable father's embrace, and Bertha sobbed with delight on her bosom!

Charlotte Maria Tucker

13. The Storm

No vain confidence hath armed me,
No presumptuous hope beguiled;

Faith in that strong love hath calmed me.
Can a sire forsake his child?

After a short and hitherto prosperous voyage, Aleck was at length drawing near to his own country, and to his delight found himself bounding over the waves of the British Channel. The depression of Mr. Brindley seemed only to increase as he approached the end of his journey, and his health appeared to benefit but little by the change of temperature and climate.

Hitherto, as I have said, the voyage had been prosperous, but the young sailor was now to see more of the works of the Lord, and his wonders in the deep.

"There'll be a pretty squall to-night!" said the boatswain, looking on the sky, where the sun was sinking beneath a heavy bank of clouds.

"Ay, ay," replied an old sailor; "if I ain't mistaken, and I've been at sea these forty and six years, we'll have more than a capful of wind afore morning."

The wind was blowing so fresh and cold that the deck was deserted by the passengers. The distant heavy nimble of thunder was heard, gradually increasing as the tempest rolled onward. The captain was more than usual on the watch, marking the approach of the storm.

The moon rose, but her pale crescent was seldom visible between the black masses of cloud which chased each other across the sky. The billows were rolling and tossing, and spreading wide their creaming foam, gleaming ghastly in the uncertain light; and the vessel plunged up and down with a laboring motion which made it difficult to keep footing on the planks. Now a huge billow dashed over the bulwarks, covering the deck with spray; another succeeded, and another, sweeping on with yet increasing fury. The gale howled and shrieked in the rigging, and the vessel seemed to reel and stagger beneath the wild force of the tempest.

Aleck had never before beheld so awful a scene. It was the first time that he had read in the hardy countenances of his messmates that anything like danger was to be apprehended. Not a eye in the ship closed in sleep during that night, and many a fervent supplication rose from it through the storm —none more fervent than that which the young sailor silently breathed, as, drenched with salt water, and almost blinded by the spray, he helped to carry into execution the captain's orders. A thought of his mother sometimes darted through his mind, a thought that it might be his fate to perish almost in sight of home, to be lost when close to the land which he had so longed to reach! But even amid the roar of the elements, the wild tumult of the storm, the voice of Faith said to the tempest tossed soul, "Be still!" The Lord was in the ship, why should the disciples fear? He would bring them safe to the haven where they would be, whether that haven were an earthly home or heaven!

The gloomy morning dawned, with no abatement of the storm. The captain had not quitted the sea-washed deck. He gave the command to heave to, with close-reefed fore and aft sails. The vessel labored heavily in the sea.

A pale, terrified face appeared just above the companion ladder. "Captain — is there danger?" gasped the voice of Mr. Brindley.

"Go down, sir!" cried the captain sternly; and at the same moment the vessel shipped a tremendous sea, which carried off part of the larboard bulwark, stove in the port-leeward life-boat, and dashed the unhappy passenger down the ladder!

Fiercer, louder howled the blast! the fore-sail was split into ribbons, the torn canvas fluttered in the gale. Another giant billow rushed over the vessel with awful force — Aleck clung to the bulwarks for life as it dashed on, smashing two boats stowed away by the main cabin hatchway, breaking the skylight, and pouring its deluge into the cabins below! Such a shriek arose as might have made the boldest heart tremble!

"She is filling — we must lighten the vessel!" The order was instantly obeyed. Casks, bales of precious goods, barrels of provisions, were cast into the raging waters as though to glut their furious thirst for destruction! A new jib was set to wear the ship, but the white fluttering canvas was instantly blown away by the gale.

The sailors were called down to the pump. Aleck worked at it with despairing energy till every muscle was strained and his strength was exhausted, and yielding his place to a hardier messmate, again he returned to his post on the deck.

"The passengers are at prayers," said one of the sailors.

"They had much need to pray," muttered the boatswain; "the water gains two feet in an hour — we can't keep her afloat till noon! "

"God have mercy upon us!" cried the sailor.

The boatswain and Aleck answered with a fervent "Amen."

Guns of distress were fired; the only hope of preservation left was that some vessel might come to the aid of the sinking ship. Eagerly, anxiously were the eyes of the crew strained in every direction; and oh! What was their relief, their joy to behold a schooner bearing down towards them — their terror lest she should not dare to venture her boats on that stormy sea!

Again looking more ghastly than ever, Mr. Drindley appeared on the deck. "Oh, tell me," He almost shrieked, as he grasped Aleck tightly by the arm, "shall we be lost? Shall we be lost?"

"There is yet hope — see, they are putting out a boat!"

"But they will be too late!" gasped the terrified man; "what if we should sink before they could reach us!"

"Sir, we are in God's hands," replied the boy.

"Yes, I know it!" cried the passenger with increasing terror; "we are in God's terrible hands — and he is the judge — the avenger! Oh! if he would grant me but life — one year — one month — I would — I would make restitution! I would give back all! Oh! Mercy, mercy!" He staggered, and sank back swooning on the deck.

The boat came nearer and nearer, plunging up and down on the waves, sometimes lost to view in the trough of the sea, then again displaying to view, as she rose, her hardy crew straining at their oars.

All the passengers were hastily summoned on deck. Shivering, trembling women, clasping children to their bosoms, and needing the support of stronger arms to enable them to stagger safely across the reeling deck, now added to the scene of wild confusion.

The captain was a brave man and true. His presence preserved something like order in the arrangements for quitting the ship; his firmness insured that a generous precedence should be given to the weak. Though it was almost momentarily expected that the vessel would settle down and sink in the waves, the gallant crew, content themselves to take the last chance, aided the women, children, and some other passengers, to make their difficult descent into the boat, which now lay alongside the ship, and cheered, like true "hearts of oak," as she sheered off again, heavy with her precious living freight.

How the minutes appeared lengthened into hours before again that boat returned on her errand of mercy! For though the fury of the tempest was abating, the Mermaid was filling fast. Again was the boat hastily filled; there was room for many, but not for all Aleck stood firmly by the side of his captain, watching her as, crowded and over laden, she heavily made her way over the turbulent waters.

"Thank God, they are safe!" murmured Aleck at last; "but we! — O heavenly Father, if thou sees good, keep this vessel afloat but for ten minutes longer; but if it be thy will that we perish, even with safety so near, enable me to die like a Christian, and comfort, oh, comfort my mother!"

Again the lightened boat rides over the waves, it comes near, Aleck hears plainly the dip of the oars, for the wind has lulled, and the thunder rolls no more. But the planks beneath him seem to shudder — to give way; there is an awful sensation of sudden sinking — the next moment he finds himself struggling, choking in the waves, drawn down into the depths with the hapless vessel!

There is a gurgling sound in his ears, a flashing before his eyes, but, with the instinct of self-preservation, he grasps a large loose spar near him, and is whirled up with it to the surface of the water. Dizzy and panting, yet his sense has not forsaken him; he sees the ex tended hand of a drowning fellow-creature, and exerting the little strength which remains to him still, Aleck seizes the hand, and draws it towards him. That one spar now supports two human forms; they cling to it as all that is between them and death, till the brave deliverers have time to row to the spot, and Aleck and Mr. Brindley are lifted into the boat, whose crew had already succeeded in picking up the noble-hearted captain!

14. The Burden That Sinks

From Nature's weeping, Earth more fair appears;
So should good works succeed repentant tears.

The exhausted sufferers were conveyed in safety to the schooner, now crowded with those rescued from the Mermaid. I need not describe the words of gratitude, the tears of thankfulness, the joyful greetings, which passed amongst those so mercifully redeemed from a watery grave. It was determined by the captain of the schooner that his vessel should put in to the nearest port on the English coast, and that there the passengers and crew of the Mermaid should be landed, to whom, in the meantime, every kindly attention was shown which circumstances permitted and their helpless condition required.

After a few hours of rest, Aleck felt his strength completely restored, and his heart swelled with strong gratitude towards his earthly deliverers, and above all to Him whose goodness had watched over the fatherless boy.

Aleck inquired for Mr. Brindley, and heard that as he was in a very weak and precarious state, the captain of the schooner had kindly allowed him the use of his own cabin, and he would not be landed with his companions. As the white cliffs of old England were now full in sight, and another hour might bring Aleck to a port, he went down to see the invalid, and to bid him farewell before quitting the schooner.

Mr. Brindley grasped his hand with intense emotion; for some moments he was too much agitated to speak. When he recovered his voice, it was not, as perhaps the youth might naturally have expected, to thank one who had been his preserver; another thought was uppermost in his mind, and his debt of gratitude appeared to be entirely forgotten.

"You said that we were in God's hands — you were right! The axe was laid to the root, but the barren tree has been spared yet another year!"

There was wildness in his eyes which made Aleck fear that his mind had been affected by the horrors through which he had passed.

"For what is it spared?" continued the sick man, attempting to raise himself on his arm, but sinking back again from exhaustion. "For what is it spared?" he repeated; and Aleck, to whom the question seemed to be addressed, but who felt embarrassed how to answer it, simply replied, "I hope for much good."

"Good — good!" repeated Brindley, bitterly; "you know not, boy, what I have on my soul. I have left God, and he now leaves me — I have sold myself for gold, and who shall redeem me back?"

"There is One who can and will redeem and save us all," exclaimed Aleck, whose strange and solemn position, bending over the sick-bed of a sinner, inspired him with courage and forgetfulness of self, and recalled to his mind exhortations which he had heard uttered by his father. "You thought that all was lost when we stood together on that sinking ship, when we every moment expected the waves to sweep over our heads; and yet the mercy of God sent deliverance. It is so with our souls: we are in danger of perishing — our own merits cannot save us — our sins are sinking us down, down to destruction; but the life-boat is coming, even in the storm — the hand of the Savior is stretched out to save us!" Brindley looked at the young speaker with a sad and earnest gaze; and then, without alluding to the effect of his words, said in a hollow tone, —

"When I knew that the ship must sink, I went into my cabin, I loaded myself with gold; I could scarcely stagger beneath the weight which I carried, but I made my way up on deck. Then, as I watched the boat from the schooner coming on her errand of mercy, and feared that our planks would give way before she had time to reach us, I thought" — he grasped Aleck's arm and drew him closer towards him, as he sank his voice to a whisper — "I thought, this gold will sink me; in God's retributive justice, his curse is upon it — it will sink me both body and soul! Roby," he added, with more animation, "I took it by handfuls and cast it into the sea; ay, every sovereign; I flung it into the depths of the sea!"

"And that was probably the reason why you were saved."

"Saved — yes!" cried the sufferer, his dim eye lighting up; "and if I cast from me the sin which still cleaves to me, weighing down the soul, clogging and destroying it, may I not still by mercy be saved indeed — saved from the deeper, darker waters of perdition!"

"I do not know what distresses your conscience thus," said Aleck; "but I am sure that God has mercy for all who repent. Has he not said. The blood of Jesus Christ his Son cleanses from all sin?"

"But can there be repentance without amendment, or amendment without restitution to those whom we have wronged?"

"No," said the young sailor at once.

"I may never be able to make restitution."

"Have you lost all your money?" said Aleck.

"No; the bulk of my fortune is in England; but I have neither seen, nor even heard of, for the last five-and-twenty years, the person whom I have cruelly defrauded. She may not be in England — she may not be in life."

"You will search for her through the world!" cried the midshipman.

"Sit down beside my cot, and Listen to me," said Brindley. "You are the first being to whom I have opened my heart; not because you have just saved my worthless life, but because you have spoken to me about my soul I will tell you all — in brief words, my guilt and my shame.

"I was brought up in the fear of God, by an aunt who loved me as a mother, and who procured for me an appointment to India. She taught me my duty — she showed me an example which would to God I had been less slow to follow! But from early years a passion for gold took possession of my heart, and, without at first knowing it, I became slave to a sin which deadens even our earthly affections, and chokes the growth of religion in the soul.

"A sweet little girl, the child of a neighbor, was a frequent visitor at the house of my aunt, a favorite of hers, and a playmate of my own, though many years younger than myself. I used to take her on my knee, to tell her stories, and amuse myself with watching her merry, artless ways.

"I always considered myself as the heir of my aunt; indeed, she made no secret of her intention of leaving to me the principal part of her little fortune. She died shortly before I sailed for India, and her will confirmed my expectations; but the property which she had left was smaller than I had imagined, and I was further surprised and annoyed to find amongst her papers a codicil, of later date than the will, leaving a legacy of five thousand pounds to the favorite child whom I have mentioned.

"I was ungenerous enough highly to resent so large a portion of what I had regarded as my own being bestowed upon one who was not even a relation. A dark thought was suggested to my mind, doubtless by him who is parent of evil —" The lawyer who drew up that codicil is now dead, no one but myself knows of its existence; it is but a piece of parchment, if I destroy it all the property if mine!"

"The fire, for it was winter-time, went crackling up the chimney; I stirred it, and watched it as it blazed up still higher. Presently the red flames were glowing round a shrinking roll; I marked it curling and blackening till a heap of ashes was all that was left to witness against me. But there is a witness within who will not be silenced. Through all these long, weary years its still, small voice has broken my rest at night and my peace by day, till during the storm it rose louder than the thunder — it was then as the trumpet which summoned me to judgment!"

"You will listen to it, you will obey its dictates!" cried Aleck; "you will restore —"

"I will restore double what I took, if ever I can discover that wronged child. But who can say that the avenging Lord will accept such tardy restitution — that it is not now too late for repentance!"

Aleck drew out a small pocket Bible, which bore signs of age and long use, and which, though it had been carefully dried, bore tokens of having been in the sea. It was the sole treasure which young Roby had saved from the ship, he having placed it in his breast to preserve it. He opened with some difficulty its leaves, which appeared as if glued together by the water, searched for the parable of the prodigal son, and then placed it silently in the hand of Mr. Brindley.

"You must have valued this Bible much said the sufferer; "you evidently carried it with you from the ship; you did not throw it away as I did the gold."

"It was my mother's when she was quite a little girl. I would not part with it for any sum of money."

Brindley sighed, and slowly with his thin languid fingers turned over to the title-page of the Bible. Then indeed he started; his whole countenance changed — his hand trembled violently, as with wild energy he exclaimed, "Whose — whose is the name written there?"

"My mother's — her name before she was married," replied Aleck, surprised at the invalid's sudden emotion.

"Thank God! I have found her — I have found her!" exclaimed Brindley; and sinking back on his pillow, the poor sufferer burst into tears!

The Battle (Illustrated)

15. Conclusion

The fairest view of Earth is given,
To him who climbs the nearest Heaven!

A changed place was Grimlee to Bertha after the step of her mother had crossed the threshold. Mrs. Roby came as the spring comes, changing, brightening, and beautifying all The aged man revived under her gentle care; he grew stronger than he had been for years. He was able, before very long, leaning on her arm, to wander into the lately neglected garden, into which Bertha, with youthful delight, was now transplanting early violets and primroses.

The season was early, and the weather charming. Soon the merry voices of singing birds were heard, the trees began to put out tender buds, little green knobs swelled on the stem of the rose-bush, and yellow crocuses laughed in the sunshine. And while everything around the house was growing fair, everything within was growing comfortable; such was the power of cleanliness, order, and good arrangement.

Bertha, before the arrival of her mother, had been shocked by tidings of the death of her poor cousin, Sam Chipstone; but though she was sincerely sorry for her aunt's heavy loss, it was not in her power very deeply to regret the resolution of the lady not to return to Grimlee. Mrs. Chipstone knew that by the death of her son the great tie was broken which had bound her to the family of her husband.

The blow which she had sustained had almost broken, but not melted her heart. She repined, she murmured, she gave way to despair; but unlike Brindley, whom she had resembled in his fault, but not in his repentance, she never searched her own spirit to discover why the judgment of the Almighty had descended upon her. Thus her tears fell as water upon a rock, — they wore a deep impression, but they brought with them no blessing;

her son had shared her affections with her gold; he was taken away, and now gold absorbed them all!

One of Mrs. Roby's earliest acts, on taking charge of the house of her venerable parent, was to make arrangements for placing with him a servant on whose ability and fidelity she could depend. She engaged the services of Susan, a valuable domestic, who had long made one of her household at Dove's Nest, and who, the lady knew from experience, was able to act, when required, the part of a nurse. When Susan was settled at Grimlee, the mind of Mrs. Roby was greatly relieved, both on the account of her father and of her child; for as spring was now far advanced, she had begun seriously to consider the expediency of her own return to London.

This was the only subject on which poor Bertha could not bear to hear her mother speak. It was a painful one to that mother, but it now occupied much of her thoughts. Her boy would soon be back from India, he would require money to support him while at home, a second outfit to prepare him for a second voyage, and a heavy fee to be paid in addition. Where was the money to come from? It is true that Mr. Chipstone's purse was in the hands of his daughter, over its contents she had unlimited command; but she would not rob him of one comfort to maintain herself and her children in idleness. No; she must again seek for a situation as governess, and once more exert herself for them all.

Mrs. Roby wrote again to her kind friend, Mrs. Lawrence, and received a most affectionate reply, but one which confirmed her in her resolution. Mrs. Lawrence told her that she was herself about to make a little tour along the south coast of England, accompanied by her beloved charge, Laura; and her nephew Constantine, now become quite a favorite, she had asked to make one of the party. They would visit Grimlee in the course of their travels, — let the children have the pleasure of meeting with Bertha, and then Mrs. Roby should return with them to London, in time to welcome home her son from the East.

Bertha would have received with unmingled delight the tidings that she was so soon to see the dear friends from whom she had been parted so long, but the idea that they would take from her mother, that she was to be the one of the circle left behind, the last to behold her darling brother, made her sorrow overpower her joy. Again a heavy sense of loneliness oppressed her, a disposition to repine, almost to rebel; but where she had before sought for comfort she sought it now — she prayed in secret for a heart more humble and resigned, and found that the prayer of faith is never in vain.

It was on a warm, sunny afternoon in April, when all nature appeared clothed in beauty, and every sound was music and joy, that Mrs. Roby ventured to place the large arm-chair in the garden, that Mr. Chipstone might enjoy the soft balmy air, and await with her and Bertha the expected arrival of the party from London. The many bees were humming amongst the flowers, the ploughman's whistle sounded cheerful in the distance; the breeze as it shook the young green leaves seemed to whisper of peace and joy. Bertha ran impatiently backwards and forwards, restless with eager expectation; while the widow, gentle and subdued, leaned on the back of the chair of her father. The old man was peacefully happy, his sunset of life unclouded and calm, not dimmed by the shadow of a care.

For the twentieth time Bertha had run to the little gate, to gaze anxiously down the dusty lane. This time a look of joy brightened her face as she cried, "Here they are! Here they are! I see them! Oh! There is Constantine standing up in the carriage! Mamma, mamma, make haste, they are coming!"

In a few minutes an open carriage dashed up to the gate; eager faces, eager hands were stretched out from it; and then there was such welcoming, such talking, such embracing and shaking of hands, while Laura skipped and danced round her sister, and Constantine laughed and would not listen to thanks, and every one seemed to have everything to say and everything to hear all in a minute, that the party appeared half wild with joy and excitement!

"How happy we are!" exclaimed little Laura, clapping her hands in an ecstasy of pleasure.

"All! If my own beloved could but have witnessed this!" thought the widow, as tears, but not sad ones, filled her eyes; "but he is happier far than even our love could have made him!"

"Oh! If Aleck were only here!" exclaimed Bertha.

"Would you welcome him?" cried a loud voice from the other side of the hedge! Bertha gave a sudden cry of joy, for she knew it; — the next moment a dusty, travel-worn figure sprang over the hedge, and Aleck was in the arms of his mother!

If the other meeting had been joyful, this was rapturous — a delight too intense for words! It was some time before Aleck could get breath to give in a few words the reason of his unexpected appearance.

"I've been shipwrecked, mother — almost lost — but God's mercy preserved me," Mrs. Roby clasped her hands.

"Oh! he must never go to sea again!" exclaimed Bertha.

"I hope not; I hope that I shall not need to do so, Bertha. I hope that I may stay at home, and be a comfort to you all — and one day, perhaps," he added in a lower tone, "enter the holy ministry Like my dear father. And mother, precious mother, shall never be a governess again — she has ten thousand pounds belonging to her at this moment!"

Laura opened both eyes and mouth wide with astonishment, Constantine whistled, Mrs. Roby and Bertha glanced at each other, half believing that Aleck's senses must be wandering; but he soon convinced them that he had spoken but truth; and oh, if ever there was a family united in love and joy and thankfulness to the Giver of all good, it was that which gathered that day in that happy home, rejoicing together in the Lord!

But a few more words, and my simple tale is ended. Another month found Mrs. Roby and her children once more in their much-loved home of Dove's Nest, that home which they had never expected to revisit again, that home endeared by so many sad yet sweet recollections! The day of their return was kept as a holiday throughout the village.

Mr. Chipstone accompanied his daughter, glad to pass the brief remainder of his days amongst those who loved him, those whom he loved.

Mrs. Lawrence, the friend in adversity, was unwilling to part with her little charge; and it was arranged that Laura should remain with her, but pass part of every year in the dwelling of her parent. "Am I not rich! I have two mammas, and two homes!" was the joyful exclamation of the child.

Constantine was invited to occupy, for as long a period as his father would permit, his old quarters in the little room at Dove's Nest; an invitation which was joyfully accepted The boy had never reason to regret his first sacrifice of selfishness to duty.

Nor was gratitude to Mr., Gruffly forgotten. His generous aid in time of need was most thankfully acknowledged, and the fee due for Aleck repaid. The ship-owner grumbled a little, in his own rough but good-humored manner, at the midshipman's change of profession "But I saw at a glance," said he, "that he was never cut out for a sailor; and he can't do better, after all, than follow in the footsteps of his father, and serve as a pilot to poor souls on their voyage to heaven!"

Mr. Brindley, who, without home or ties, felt reluctant to be separated from Aleck, to whom circumstances had so strangely united him, took a lodging at a neighboring farmer's, and was a frequent visitor at Dove's Nest. There, where the world and its temptations seemed almost excluded, his broken and contrite spirit found rest; his health both of body and mind was restored; and the poor of the parish, relieved by his bounty, little guessed that their generous benefactor had once been a slave to the love of gold! He resolved to defray all the expenses of Aleck's education, and, when the youth was old enough, to send him to college, that he might prepare to enter the ministry, so long the object of his heart's desire.

Thus did the penitent sinner endeavor to bring forth fruits meet for repentance, ever humbled under a sense of his own unworthiness, but cheered by the hope of pardon and acceptance held out to him in the Sacred Volume; for he had learned to wield the sword of the Spirit, that which is alike powerful in our conflict against trials from without and temptations from within

The heart knoweth his own bitterness, and a stranger doth not intermeddle with his joy, but the blessed remedy for the one, the true source of the other, are to be found in the Word of God.

THE END

Made in the USA
Las Vegas, NV
29 June 2024